MW00939768

RAVAGE MC REBELLION BOOK ONE

CONNECTED
IN
pain

CROW & RYLYNN TRILOGY

RYAN MICHELE

Copyright ©Connected in Pain 2018 Ryan Michele—Wicked Words Publishing LLC

All Rights Reserved. This literary work may not be reproduced or transmitted in any form or by any means, including electronic or photographic reproduction in whole or in part, without express written permission from Ryan Michele.

This is a work of fiction. All characters, organizations, and events portrayed in this novel are either products of the author's imagination or are used fictitiously. Any resemblance to actual events, locales, or persons, living or dead, is entirely coincidental.

This work of fiction is intended for mature audiences only. All sexually active characters portrayed in this book are eighteen years of age or older. Please do not buy if strong sexual situations, violence and explicit language offends you.

This is not meant to be an exact depiction of life in a motorcycle club, but rather a work of fiction meant to entertain.

1st edition published: November 6, 2018

ASIN: B07FKZMT5K

ISBN: 9781730936562

Editing by: Silla Webb at Masque of the Red Pen

Cover Design by: Cassy Roop at Pink Ink Designs

Photography by: Wander Aguiar at Wander Aguilar Photography

Models: Nathan Van Dyken

BLURB

Rylynn

Beauty in the pain, that saying was a crock of shit.

Life doesn't give you more than you can handle, that saying was a lie.

I knew life. I knew love. I knew family.

I knew loss.

I knew *pain*.

My life was the Ravage MC.

Nothing would ever be the same, though.

I didn't like change.

I was restless... seeking something I would never find.

Crow

I knew freedom. I knew family. I knew loyalty.

Then I learned the truth.

Find healing in the pain, they said. That was bullshit.

They didn't know my story.

They didn't know her story.

They damn sure didn't know our story.

She was my truth in the web of lies. She was my strength and my biggest weakness. She was the first person I ever held who meant more than my cut.

We were connected in pain, bound by loyalty, and consumed in lust. Somehow, we had to sort through where we came from to find where we would be going... whether that was together or apart.

Welcome to Ravage MC, Rebellion Chapter.

Ride free.

To my Mom
You are the strongest woman I know.
The last few months you've fought, always laughing and spirits so damn high every step of the way, you're an inspiration.
Love you.
Always and forever.
~M

PROLOGUE

Crow

THE CALM BEFORE THE CHAOS.

A moment to shut the world out.

The pavement passing beneath my tires.

Nothing but me, the wind, and my machine.

This moment and the many like it before were personal times to find peace in the pain, clarity in the confusion, and a way to clear the clutter of my mind.

Pipes rumbled down the long stretch of road, tires eating up the distance as the yellow lines passed under me in a blur. Heat pressed in from the sun above, the wind the only thing cooling my heated flesh. This was my favorite expanse of highway—off the beaten path, yet not. Close to home, yet not. The twists called to me like a red flag to a bull, challenging me and allowing me to just be free.

Free.

It was exactly what being a biker was about. Freedom from society's expectations. Freedom from being boxed into someone's ideals of what a man should do or be. Riding was allowing yourself to feel the elements, experience every bump, every curve, and every clearing.

The gravel under me moved behind me like all the thoughts in my mind. Clearing my head sometimes was difficult, much like this road could be at times.

The weight of the world laid heavily on my shoulders. So many things felt like they were coming at me from different ends, life spinning around not allowing me to just take a moment to stop and breathe. There was no extra time to think out what needed to happen and what needed to be done to get that result. Making decisions on the fly was something I excelled at, but sometimes I just needed that break from everything around me to allow my head to release and recharge.

When all the thoughts piled up, I needed the freedom only the open road could give me.

Hands on the bars, my body vibrated becoming one with the machine. With each rev of the engine, every curve of the road, every change of the gears, my mind settled breaking into a calm I could only get from riding. The Harley Davidson Road King had the miles under her leaving her engine fine tuned to a sweet hum. Over the years she'd had parts added, parts removed, things customized, but my 1995 ride was still a heavy beast with a black paint job and red ghosted skulls airbrushed onto the gas can. While I had owned other bikes, and will have many more in the future, this bitch under me was my first.

Loved my bike. Loved my club. Loved it more than words could say. Even loved the shit that came with it. But every man needed a break now and then. A way to put everything in your life into perspective and allow yourself that time.

These rides alone were mine.

Only mine.

There was little in life I had to claim as solely mine. My life was this club, Ravage. It was a choice I made knowing full and well I was giving everything I had to give to this world, this family. Every moment, I had to be ready to drop whatever I had going on for the club, and I would.

Still, though, I took this ride and many like it to decompress. Sure, some people didn't understand it, couldn't understand me, but I didn't give a fuck.

While my brothers wanted to be alongside me to show our solidarity and I appreciated it, this was something that had to be done on my own. A time out of sorts for my soul. They didn't have the responsibilities of being the president in the Ravage MC and having the final say in all decisions and making sure they were the right ones.

It was a balancing act to keep everyone and everything in line. Money, time, businesses, allies, enemies, brothers, hell life itself—all of it laid on a tight rope just waiting for me to misstep and topple over, taking my club down with me. Not that I'd ever let that shit happen. It was something to keep a tight hold on, which was what I did, how I rolled. It was why I rode every now and then, on this stretch of road, completely alone.

Peace.

The '*Welcome to Rebellion*' sign passed by telling me I was home.

Who the fuck would name a town Rebellion?

Often times, we all sat back and laughed at the thought of it.

Rebellion, Alabama. Crazy name for a town.

It fit us, though.

Rebels with a cause or more like a mission. A solid foundation to build. That was us. All of us. My club, my people, and fuck anyone who got in the way of either.

This was where I ran the show, held the power, had respect, and with that came responsibilities.

Adulting sucked for some men.

Yeah, back in the day I never thought this would be me. My focus was different. Even young I had responsibilities. Ravage needed me to have a solid head on my shoulders, needed me to have a firm grip on who I was. This club made me the man I was today, modeling and shaping me to be the president of the club.

Driving into town the hustle and bustle of everyday life surrounded me. The calm I just found would soon disappear as the thoughts would crowd my mind once again much like the people on the go in Rebellion. People going to work in suits and ties while others were in uniforms. Everyone wanting to get somewhere as fast as possible without having to wait for anyone.

Most of them not knowing how the world really works, we took on the responsibility of keeping Rebellion, Alabama under our control.

Because of the chaos of the streets, I made a change for this ride and went around the town, down the backroads, and came up from the opposite way seeing the clubhouse on my left. Those few, extra precious moments to let myself simply *be* had me ready to take on the world once again.

One couldn't see into our space through the tall metal structures that outlined the acres of land we owned. All they could see was pole barn metal, not the thick cinderblocks behind it giving us security. If someone tried running into it, they'd get a very rude awakening.

The gate was automatic and with a touch of a button from Ethan, a prospect, up in the tower above the wall, it would open wide. There was a walkway above the gate from one end to the other made of bulletproof glass allowing whoever was on watch to see all around them. We took our security very seriously because of the shit we were into.

There was a time we didn't and paid a fuck of a price for it. That shit wouldn't happen again.

Ethan lifted his chin, and the sun glistened off the gate as it moved to the side allowing me access inside.

This was where I was meant to be.

This was where I belonged.

Refreshed, I was back and on fire. Let's fuckin' do this shit.

Welcome to Ravage Rebellion.

1

Rylynn

Pain.

I knew that shit well.

Not right now though. No, right now I was lost and in far too deep, but not lost in the pain for once since everything happened. It was a foreign feeling to not be wrapped in the darkness, the sorrow that had become my life.

I felt lost and found all at the same time.

Confusion, that was some of it. I was disorientated in a blissful way that was unusual for me.

My mouth tasted of cotton that had been up a monkey's ass and my head throbbed like a village of ants playing the bongos, but that was a pain I could deal with. Too much booze did that to a woman, especially when she'd lost someone she loved. My head was normally screwed on pretty tight, but not last night, because I had to let loose. I couldn't stay in the pain, stay in the emotions. I needed to escape. I had to get every miniscule feeling out because it'd been bottled up and waiting to explode, tearing me apart and eating at my insides for days now.

Nothing tore me apart. Nothing.

I was unshakable. Unbreakable.

At least, that was what I'd thought.

I was Rylynn Cameron Hutton. The daughter of Rhys and Tanner. Granddaughter of Dagger and Mearna. Sister of Mazie.

We didn't break. It wasn't in our DNA. We were taught to be strong and unfuckable. To ride the road of life with all the twists and turns of it not once letting go of that strength.

Life proved me wrong, though, with the death of my grandpa.

It was my kryptonite.

My family would never be whole again. A member of it no longer on this planet. It killed me and inside I was hollow, part of my soul forever gone. I felt the missing piece down to the core of my being. Every breath felt wrong, disconnected, like I was here but I wasn't and nothing was right.

How were we supposed to go on? Every morning I woke feeling like maybe, just maybe, it was all a bad dream. Only I would look at my phone, call his number, and the same generic message met me every single time.

I missed his voice.

I missed his smell.

I missed his wisdom.

I missed him.

It killed me inside and out. I would never be the same without him. We would never be the same. Our worlds shattered into a million and one pieces, never to be complete again. The strength we had was being tested. We needed it now more than ever.

Going after the assholes who did this wasn't an option for me. It was stated it was club business, and it took everything inside of me to refrain from looking because I wanted to tear them apart from limb to limb. The need for revenge rode me hard with every passing second, and keeping a hold on that proved difficult. Not impossible, but hard as hell.

Last night, the bourbon was great going down to drown my sorrow, but now—now, not so much. My head swam, thumped, and throbbed, my stomach roiling and wanting to expel. Fuck, how much did I drink last night?

Oh right. A bottle of bourbon with no chaser. If anything would do it, that would.

Even with the cotton mouth, the constant drumming, and the way my eyes couldn't quite focus, for a moment last night, for a short bit of time, I forgot to feel.

I didn't feel the loss.

I didn't feel the gaping hole in my heart.

I didn't feel one thing.

All I felt was each shot hitting the back of my throat as the alcohol warmed going down before settling deep in my belly. Every bit allowing the pain to be pushed away further and further, giving me a reprieve.

The cool air hit my skin, and I looked down noting my naked, nearly uncovered body, my calves the only thing the sheet hid. Even with the grogginess, last night crashed into me, visions flashing before my eyes, my body starting to heat at the thoughts.

The touches, kisses, caresses, unbelievable. I turned...

Crow laid next to me, sheet at his waist displaying his heavily tattooed arms and chest which were seriously defined. His face turned the other way giving me views of his sandy brown hair. Hair that was messed up due to my fingers twisting and pulling it during our marathon session last night.

Fuck me.

Guess if you're gonna fuck up, may as well go big or go home.

I did.

Fucking the president of the Rebellion chapter of the Ravage MC was a huge mistake, and the first time I'd ever slept with a brother, something I swore to myself I'd never do. Growing up in this life I'd seen so much and I never wanted to have the title of *that one girl that one night*, but I guessed it was under my belt now and there was no going back.

Of all the guys in the club, it had to be *him* of all people. I was out of my mind.

Hot, sexy as hell, rough, take no shit—Crow.

Fuck, even his damn name was mysterious and foreboding, leading me thousands of ways in how to interpret. Too bad I didn't ask him how he got his road name, or I assumed it was his road name because not many men would be named Crow, but who the hell knew anymore.

We were too busy doing other things to discuss the intricacies of his name.

Great things.

Sexy things.

Hot things.

Things that didn't involve conversations about names or pretty much anything. Movement, noises of pleasure, and the air conditioner kicking on then off were the only sounds in the room.

I was an idiot even if I still felt him between my

thighs in delicious ways. But the worst part was *I* put myself in this position. He kept looking at me across the room at the clubhouse, and I approached him. No, I couldn't believe it either, but I did. One touch of those sensuous lips of his and I melted. The rest was obviously history.

Searching the room for the time, I took in the space, needing to get my head out of the clouds and get focused. The layout was like any other hotel I'd ever been in: bed, TV, dresser, chair and desk. The sleek lines of silver around the mirror and accents of the furniture screamed of money. That could only mean one thing—we were at the Marriot right outside of Sumner, Georgia about twenty-five miles from my home.

Shit.

Too close, but still far away.

Since Crow gave me a ride last night on the back of his bike, now I had to figure out how in the hell to get home from here. Another stupid move, but being on the back while he drove the roads of my hometown with the moon shining down on us last night was incredible and worth every second of it. The getaway portion of the morning though, not having my Jeep was a hindrance. But I was a big girl and could handle anything life threw at me. That was what we did in my family. Problem, find a solution. End of story.

Being around clubs all my life, I knew how this

one-night stand situation worked. *Brother picked up a woman, fucked her seven ways to Sunday, then kicked her out on her ass after he had his fill.*

A piece of ass.

Fuck, now I was one of them, something I never wanted to be in the club life. Women were all over the guys in the club before they met their significant others. They did the fuck-n-go on more than one occasion, never even remembering the chick's name. Hell, Cooper and Ryker tore up the sheets all the damn time. Not now, though. Now, I was the one doing it. No, I chose to do it. Had no one to blame but my damn self for putting me smack dab in the center of the situation.

Seemed my thoughts of staying clear from being one of those girls went up in a huge puff of smoke. Lost in a blur of alcohol, a haze of pain, I allowed myself to fall to the very depths of Hell with a man I could tell would show me a great time. Shit, I initiated it, even going as far as kissing him right off the bat with no preamble or small talk whatsoever.

The strange thing was that after those thoughts swam through my head, I searched for the guilt that I thought would smear my conscience.

Guilt that I went against my own damn rule.

Guilt that I slept with someone from my father's club.

Guilt that I knew the hurtful look in so many women's eyes the morning after.

Except that look wasn't on my face. That wasn't what I had inside me.

The feeling of regret wasn't showing its ugly head, chasing me down with a crowbar ready to beat the shit out of me.

Except that emotion wasn't there barreling through, trying to take over my rational thoughts. There was no resentment for what I'd done or being angry with myself. Crow helped kill the pain last night, exactly what I'd needed to keep going. There was no way to get pissed at that. He gave me what I needed more times than I could count, taking me away from life for a period of time.

A steel tattooed, banded arm fell across my stomach pulling me into Crow's hard and warm, just woke from sleep body, my head having no choice but to fall on the pillow next to his as he'd turned his body some time during my thoughts.

Damn, the man was strong. We'd battled it out last night, each of us wanting the upper hand and each wanting to be in control of the night. Unfortunately, with him being built with hard muscle, fast reflexes, and being all man, he took me over with frustrating ease, even with my best defensive moves and I had an arsenal of them. It was sexy as all hell when he brought me to surrender, because not many could do that, and it kicked ass that for the first time in my life

Crow was able to accomplish it in the most delicious of ways.

"Kiss," he ordered, his lips coming in to claim mine, and immediately I pulled back. No way in hell he was coming near my mouth before a toothbrush went through it—twice. No man wanted to taste cotton mouth from the chick he fucked the night before. That was just gross. Fuck, I didn't want to taste that shit either, but was stuck for the moment.

His brow raised in question, but he said nothing waiting for me to explain. This was one of the swift revelations when it came to Crow. He had this way about him, that he didn't need to say a word, but you knew he wanted more information. You would think it'd be obvious what my dilemma was for him, but apparently not and I needed to fill in the gaps.

"Bourbon tastes like sweaty balls after a workout at the gym in the morning, buddy."

A slow, sexy smirk tipped the corners of his lips, my body wanting to pull even closer to him. That one movement was such a dynamic change to his hard face that part of me melted. The man was gorgeous in that rough, *don't fuck with me, I'll beat the living shit out of you if you come near me*—way. A look that made my body alert and wanton. There was no doubt in my mind that if someone was on Crow's bad side, they wouldn't last long on this planet.

He in no way took me for a man to put up with shit

and eat it. Instead, a man who would do what needed to be done without hesitation.

But that damn smirk was killer. It pulled me in like no other and if I didn't have sweaty balls in my mouth, my lips would be on his in a flash.

Crow didn't speak. Quick as lightning though, he released me, his arms wrapping around my spread opened thighs, his body falling to his stomach positioning right at my core where his mouth attacked. Speedy. Fuck, he was fast for a big guy. The way he had control of his body was damn impressive.

"What are you—" My words were cut off when his tongue flicked my clit and sent spasms up my spine, causing me to arch at the sensations. His tongue felt rough over my flesh one moment, then soft the next. He repeated this over and over, changing it up.

"Having breakfast," he said, but I really didn't care because he was devouring me with his mouth, his lips pulling in as he sucked my hard nub. My hands went to the sheets and dug into the softness, holding on for dear life as if my fingertips would stop me from floating from this spot up into the air.

Crow was damn good with his mouth, like he should get an award for 'fastest and most precise tongue flicks' because he knew exactly when to give them to me, at what speed and what pressure. Even going as far as to give it circles that ended in a deep suck. As I looked down, his blue eyes captured mine, holding me captive in some sort of trance and causing me to be unable to look away.

He was reading me, my body, taking notes on what got me off and what didn't. Which part of my pussy got the most reaction and experimenting with his fingers this way and that to find just the right spot to set me aflame. The ways my body arched or quivered and doing those things over and over again like the tempo of a song on repeat. If something didn't get the reaction out of me that he wanted, he changed it up to something new, never stopping, never giving me a second to gather myself, keeping me on edge, making me yearn for it. My head flew back to the bed.

His fingers inside of me crooked up rubbing the sensitive flesh, building my body higher and higher. My skin was hot and a slight sheen came over it holding nothing back from this man, letting him see exactly how he made me feel. I couldn't. My body wouldn't allow it. Instead, it was pushing me, taunting me, and making me crave more and more, pushing me to want to beg for his cock. I didn't beg, but fuck if I didn't for want to for him. He was that damn good.

My clit spasmed as he flicked then sucked it, doing this while his fingers thrust in and out of me, rubbing the sensitive walls.

All of it together was too much.

Too much feeling.

Too much winding up.

Too much everything.

Clutching the sheets and pulling them from the confines of the mattress, my body bucked when wave after wave of pleasure swept through every cell inside of me exploding me into particles in the atmosphere. My mind blanked letting this moment sweep me away and ride the euphoria, my body shaking on its own accord. Yeah, staying here until the end of time would be fantastic.

He was damn good at this beginning to know my body more than myself.

Crow didn't stop touching, licking, kissing and sucking as my mind started to float back down to earth, my body becoming flush on the bed once again. The light sheen of sweat turned into full wetness, my arm going to my forehead to wipe it away quickly. Working out today wouldn't be necessary. Crow took care of that just fine.

Breaths were hard to intake. Once I pulled my shit together and was able to steady myself, my eyes gazed down at him. He gave my mound one more kiss, lifted up, and gave me the killer smile that landed my ass here in the first place.

That alone was a weapon.

Lethal. Brutal. Beautiful.

The first one I saw at the clubhouse wasn't even directed at me, but it hit me between the legs rocking my world on its axis and bringing me here.

"Smug," I murmured, my head falling down to the bed missing the pillow and collapsing on the mattress. When he said nothing for a moment, I lifted up on my elbows to look down at him, but the moment my arms touched the mattress, hands went around my ankles and pulled me down the bed.

An unexpected shriek filled the air when Crow lifted me as if I weighed nothing and carried me to the bathroom, setting me on my feet. The cool tile did nothing to alleviate the warmth coursing through me. Good thing his arm was around my waist because the quick movement had my brain screaming at me to take it easy. "What are you doing?"

Crow said nothing.

A man of few words I was coming to realize, but as I stared at him, he said, "Teeth" and he pointed to the sink, then leaned into my ear, his lips caressing the shell. "Our tongues'll be dancin'."

Damn that was hot. The few words he spoke packed a hell of a punch. My knees felt wobbly for a moment before I stopped that shit and stared at him in the mirror. "Smoke signals would've worked better."

His brow quirked as I knew it would. The sarcasm that came from my lips was something people around me either loved or hated. Most saw it as a bitch thing, while others laughed and caught on quickly. Some people had sticks up their asses and didn't get me, which was fine because I didn't want to get them either.

They weren't my kind of people, which were a select few in this world.

His teeth nipped my ear and warned, "Thirty seconds."

"I hear cotton mouth is the new thing. All the chicks are trying it."

He said nothing again, just stared at me through the mirror, waiting, but not really waiting... more like challenging me. Which I didn't get, but I was no pussy. I may have one, but that didn't mean I was one. Two completely different things.

I kept his stare meeting his invitation.

"Fifteen." His fingertips dug into my hips, biting into my flesh. Crow was on edge, his eyes filled with desire, and I was going to push him over. I couldn't help myself.

"Threw up a little in the night too. Add that to cotton and you've got a party in my mouth."

That didn't faze him in the least because he smirked just waiting for me again, saying nothing.

It occurred to me that I had set up the rules. It was me who told him not to kiss me because the taste was gross. It wasn't him because he was obviously fine with it and wanted it before the words left my lips.

He didn't tell me *I* had to do anything. He brought me into the bathroom because of me saying I needed to brush. This had nothing to do with him and everything to do with me. Crow was doing me a solid, giving me what I'd asked for. Dammit.

"Seven," he warned, and I grabbed the ugly as hell complimentary white toothbrush and paste, then brushed the hell out of my teeth, repeating the process twice. I spit, tried to grab a towel to wipe off my mouth, but it was no use because Crow's lips were on mine.

My taste on his tongue turned me on and damn him, there wasn't a hint of morning breath or cotton mouth to be found on him. How the hell did guys do that? Still taste damn good after a night of drinking and fucking. Women, at least me, weren't that lucky.

He stole my breath, my hands moving up to thread through his hair at the nape as he pulled me as close to him as possible. His hands went to my ass, lifting me up as my legs wrapped around his hard, naked hips. My breasts pressed into him, nipples becoming aroused peaks. Wetness pooled at my thighs as I rubbed my clit on him like a fucking cat in heat.

One explosive orgasm only moments ago and I was ready to go again. Damn this man.

His hands squeezed my ass hard, to the point of erotic pain. I ripped my lips from his and yelled out, tossing my head back as my hips ground more into his abs craving the friction. Shit, I was almost there and he wasn't even inside me.

Crow walked me out of the bathroom and my back found the bed, his hard cock at my entrance ready to plunge inside and I wanted it, desperately. Needed it. Craved it.

One solid thrust and he was deep inside of me, my body stretching to accommodate him and burning at the same time. He wasn't my first, but he was the first with this much girth and I felt him everywhere, opening me and making me burst from the seams. It was so damn good.

My legs wrapped around his hips and tightened and flexed with each of his movements, while his lips came down on mine and sucked what little air I had in my lungs out. His back was covered in a slight sheen as his hips went to work pounding inside of me. The cords of his muscular arm flexed with each of his thrusts.

Crow pulled out, my eyes flying open to stare at his blues. A wicked grin tilted his lips as he flipped me to my belly then climbed on top of me and pressed my legs together. I couldn't think or move because he had me captured, pinning me to the bed with his weight.

His knees wide over my hips, he tipped my hips just a touch and found my entrance once again. This position was indescribably deeper, and a cry poured out when he touched my womb. Each stroke of him in that spot sent me higher and higher. It was as if it were another G-spot or something up there and with the combination of my clit rubbing against the sheets and his cock not slowing, I dropped my head to the mattress and screamed out my release.

"Fuck your pussy," he grunted it like a curse, his hips pistoning like an engine, the bed hitting the wall and making a steady rhythm of noise that I didn't give one shit if someone was pissed in the next room for.

My orgasm continued or maybe another one hit, I wasn't sure, but my body was loving every second of the thrill of the ride.

On an intense upward thrust, he stilled inside and I could feel his cock pulsing, spilling himself inside of me. Fuck, I needed to get to the pharmacy and get the morning after pill. He fucked me all night without a condom, and I hadn't said a damn word. I'd had an IUD for years, but fucking him raw was a mistake. Fucking any man you didn't plan on being in your bed regularly wasn't smart to do ungloved, and the morning after pill would just give me more reassurance that at least a baby wouldn't be in the mix.

Ungloved. Mark this in the stupid as fuck category. Bikers didn't have a code for getting off, but most did have one for using condoms considering the amount of ready pussy available to them. That was my own fault though, because I was smarter than that and wanted to kick my own ass for it. Doctor's appointment would be in my future. He'd better be clean or I'd have to shoot that gorgeous dick off, and that would be a shame for all womankind.

His weight came down on my back, his labored breathing all I could feel. Lips came to my ear with the pants sending chills down my spine making me feel wonderful that I put this strong man to the point of exhaustion. Already warm, his hard body made me feel like an inferno burning from the inside out. Normal was never my thing, but being ready to go again right after fucking someone's brains out was a bit over the top. But here I was ready for more.

It was such a turn on that he wanted me so badly, like he couldn't get enough of me. He craved me. Wanted me. And that feeling was mutual. The chemistry between us could cause more sparks than a fireworks show.

He was so fucking good at this, but being older than me he'd for sure had his fair share of practice. I didn't know exactly how old he was, but I knew it was older than Cooper. So, my guess was early thirties. Really though, who gave a shit? Age was just a number to tick off on your paperwork. It didn't mean anything in the grand scheme of life. He may have more experience than me, but fuck yeah, I could hold my own.

"Fuck, Ry," he groaned, pulling out of me and rolling to the bed on his back. I took that opportunity to roll to mine and get some fresh air inside my lungs and on my body.

"Not so bad yourself for an old guy," I teased.

His head turned to me, brow lifted. "I'll fuckin' show you old."

He rolled me over and proceeded to show me—twice more—how old he was, and I loved every second of it.

Rules be damned, I fucked myself this time as hard as he fucked me.

2

Crow

HOW THE FUCK WAS MY COCK HARD AGAIN, JUST FROM laying by Rylynn? That shit hadn't happened since I was a fucking teen when pussy was all I thought about. With Ry though, I didn't think the sated feeling would ever come. It was strange to feel this way. I wasn't used to it. Nor had it ever happened before.

The way she rode me last night, no inhibitions and so one with her body and mind—every second such a fucking turn on. She knew what she wanted, how to get it, and didn't hesitate with me. She went after her pleasure, and it was fun as hell to take her over.

Hell, everything about her had my cock springing to attention and wanting more of her. Any part of her. Watching her drown her grief in a bottle of bourbon last night, I told myself to stay the fuck away. Not my gig to fuck a woman who was drowning her sorrows no matter if she made my cock twitch from the sight of her. It didn't mean that I couldn't keep my eyes off her, though. Fuck, she was so damn hot she burned the damn floor with each step she took.

Then she approached me, hips swaying, lip tipped and every thought of keeping a distance flew out the fucking window, taking a long ass road trip. When she lifted on her tiptoes and pressed her lips to mine bold as you please, that was it. I had to have her in every damn way possible.

Unfortunately, time was our enemy and getting everything I wanted to do to that beautiful body wasn't going to be easy, but I'd damn well try; once I caught my breath that is.

My brothers and I needed to ride out today and get back to Alabama. Shit needed to be done at home. Shit always needed to be done at home, but fuck me I could lay in this bed all day and not allow her to come up for air.

Immediately after that thought, my phone rang, the tone of Brewer, my VP. Fuck. Time was officially up. Rylynn tensed beside me, more than likely knowing the same thing I did. She said nothing, just laid there, her tits pert and standing at attention. Fuck, she had sexy tits, so big and fucking real. There was absolutely no fake anywhere on Rylynn.

Snatching the phone, I swiped it to answer. "Crow."

"Brother," Brewer said with no preamble. "Where the fuck are you? We're ready to roll out." Turning to the clock, it read eleven thirty. We were supposed to meet up at noon to leave. Fuck, I was going to be late.

"Be there in an hour. Have somethin' to do." I disconnected after his *later*.

Tossing the phone back to the nightstand with a clatter, I rolled into Rylynn's warm, sated, soft body wanting nothing more than to sink back inside and kiss every inch of her body over and over again. Instead, responsibilities meant leaving. "Gotta go."

Her smile knocked me on my ass, so wide and bright. She was sunshine beneath all the dark clouds pushing the ugly away to let her brightness through. It took me aback wanting that feeling never to end. It was a gift, one she didn't know she was giving.

The darkness of my life at times overshadowed everything. Getting that from Rylynn was a breath of fresh air.

"Know that." Her hand came up to cup the side of my face in a very comforting gesture, putting me off guard, but I wasn't sure why I felt that way. Maybe it was the moment or the soft look in her eyes, or maybe it was just her.

"Get dressed and I'll take you home."

She stared up at me, her eyes now dancing with something I couldn't nail down. Fuck, they were so damn expressive as if she had nothing to hide and showed herself off to the world.

"I'm good. I know my way home."

Stubborn. That's what she was, and no fucking way was I letting her get herself home with no ride. Fuck if she was going to call a damn Uber or some shit. Let alone walk home. No, not happening.

"Get dressed and I'll take you home." The growl caught her attention, but the smile only widened making me want to pull her in closer but I was on top of her; couldn't get much closer than that except inside her, and there wasn't time.

She got off on giving me shit, and fuck if that didn't turn me on. Anyone else would get a bullet between the eyes, yet Rylynn could do it every minute of the day and I'd welcome it.

"You really should tone down the growl, Grizzly." Her voice deepened. "Only you can protect forest fires."

Fuck, she was funny. That smart little mouth on her was something I didn't expect, but liked it. A lot. Probably a bit too much. And the fact that I didn't give a shit that she called me Grizzly and not Crow wasn't my style. With her though, it was like another gift somehow. Her giving me something that was just between her and I. Fuck, I was going to end up getting my balls cut off if this kept up.

"Don't got time to show you the fire, Pixie. Get your ass moving," I said, rolling off the bed to stand beside her and grabbing my clothes.

She shifted off. "Pixie? How the hell do you think that name fits me?"

This made me chuckle as I got dressed. Rylynn was the furthest thing from a pixie being around five-ten or five-eleven. She was tall for a woman, and it was all legs. They went on for fucking miles, thought for sure they'd wrap around my back twice when I fucked her.

Then there was the fact that she had a smart mouth she used regularly. Therefore, I named her Pixie because why the fuck not even if it's the total opposite for her. It made the entire thing work. If I was Grizzly, she was Pixie.

She got tired of waiting for me to answer, shook her head and said, "Pixie my ass," bending down to grab her jeans and pull them on.

"Your legs, babe. All fuckin' legs," I responded, putting my leather cut on my back as she slipped on her boots. The jeans she had on completely gave every bit of truth to my words. The way they hugged her ass and accentuated her hips and legs made my mouth water to kiss and nip.

"Aren't they great?" she said, not missing a beat, sticking her legs out and showing them off.

I burst out laughing, that damn sharp tongue of

hers, as she continued. "My ass too." Ry turned around giving me a view of her ass as she looked down at it giving it a small bounce. My cock jerked.

"Don't got time to fuck you."

Her face twisted humorously. "Pity." She threw her mass of blonde hair on top of her head and tied a band around it, pieces going every which way. Even that was hot, all the thick shininess confined and ready to be pulled while I fucked her. Coming up on her, I wrapped my arms around tight and pulled her to my body kissing her hard, wet, and deep, needing that contact from her.

Not once while with Rylynn did the weight of life try to crush me. Just being in the same room as her I didn't feel it. It was something I only got on the open road, but here in a hotel in Georgia, she'd given it to me freely. Fuck. How many times had there been when I couldn't get away from the woman in my bed fast enough? Now with Rylynn it was the complete opposite.

She relaxed into me, her hands going to the nape of my neck then to my hair. When I pulled back and looked into her eyes, I wished I could stay just a few more days—work her out of my system. Explore her. Do all the things I was dying to with her. Have her on her knees in front of me taking my cock. Fuck her against the wall. Spank her ass red then fuck her until she screamed. Have everything inside of my head calm and become clearer because she could do it with a look.

But we would part here and go on with our lives. Her life was here in Sumner. Mine was in Rebellion. Life was life, and it took you on different paths. Our time was up. It was a fucking great one.

"Come on. Let me take you home." Her head shook as she smiled, stepping back and grabbing her bag. Her ass swayed all the way to the elevator, to my bike, and once on her pussy was hot on my ass. Fuck.

The ride to her place wasn't long, maybe twenty minutes. She used her fingers to point what direction to turn. Her arms were wrapped tight around me the other times, her tits pressed to my back. My damn cock was hard as a rock once again feeling her heat all around me. There wasn't time for another round. Another chance to be inside the sweetest pussy I'd ever tasted. The club always came first, and my brothers were waiting as it was.

Pulling up, I took in the large building. It was three stories high covered in a light green siding. The front of the building had three separate entrances labeled with letters making it clear it was an apartment complex.

With the manicured lawns, marked parking, and cameras on the outside of the building, it was what I would consider upscale for the average person. It was obvious Rylynn was younger than me, but gauging her place, I would guess she had to be in her mid-twenties in order to afford this on her own. Reading people, I did it often needing to know everything around me to stay alive. The read I got on Rylynn was she wasn't the kind of woman to let anyone pay her way in life.

A strong woman taking care of business, that was a fucking turn on. Not that I wasn't already rock fucking hard. Now, it pressed so tight against my zipper it was sure to leave impressions. Dammit.

I shut down the bike, flipping down the kickstand, and looked at my watch. It told me I needed to get a move on for the guys, so any plans of a quick fuck at her place wouldn't be happening even if I thought about it the entire ride.

Club before pussy.

Always.

Rylynn swung her leg over the bike and hopped off like a pro definitely knowing her way around a steel machine. She leaned over and kissed my lips quickly. "Thanks for the ride, Grizzly."

This made me chuckle. Wrapping my hand around her neck, I pulled her in tight, kissing her hard one last time and taking everything possible from her and giving just the same. "Take care of yourself, Rylynn."

She smiled, and it beamed like a strobe light. "Always. Same with you."

Rylynn didn't wait for me to start the engine. Instead, she turned and took off inside the building. Once the middle door was shut, I took off to find my brothers.

Time waited for no one, not even a fucker like me.

3

Crow

"TELL ME WHAT THE FUCK HAPPENED?" MY TONE WAS clipped because I was fucking pissed. No, more than pissed—fucking livid.

"Prosecution pulled up some trumped up evidence to say it was premeditated. They just threw it on the table today," Kevin, the club's newest lawyer said, looking me square in the eye, but there was a small tick at his temple telling me that it was taking everything inside of him not to flinch.

Smart man.

"What evidence?"

"They didn't give specifics," he answered, still holding his ground. "There is a process, you have to understand that," he began to explain, and I threw my hand up silencing him. Fuck the process, I didn't want to hear that shit. Ravage had their own *process.* It was called *get my fucking brother out of the joint before you end up six feet under* process.

"You gonna be able to make this go away?" I asked, crossing my arms over my chest as we stood outside the clubhouse, under the sun in the parking lot. The last guy didn't and paid the price for it.

Kevin never made it inside the clubhouse because as soon as he stepped foot on Ravage property, I stormed out to meet him. This was too important to waste the precious seconds it would take him to get to me. I was fine with our meeting in the parking lot. He needed to get shit done not waste time walking and talking. He knew I was already pissed from his phone call not twenty minutes ago, and nothing had changed in those minutes. Controlled rage was what my father called it.

It was a skill. Keeping it controlled was difficult at times, but in my line of work, no control got you killed.

"Gotta see what they have and go from there."

He was definitely a smart man. Telling me what I needed to hear and yet giving me nothing. True lawyer speak. No promises, yet keeping everything open to possibilities. I knew his fucking game, and I wasn't playing it.

I leaned in close making Kevin's body stiffen. The fear was trying to take him over, but he forced it to recede. That, I respected a little. "Make sure this shit goes away and our boy comes home. Don't give a fuck how that happens, but that's the outcome."

Unfortunately, punching him in the temple wouldn't speed up the process here, even if he needed to be laid the fuck out. This was me. I had to think every move out. I hit him, well, then we'd have to cover the hospital bills because I couldn't kill him... yet. Right now, he had a job to do and to do it, he needed to have his brain intact and not jumbled into mush by my fists.

Rook, one of our brothers, had been in prison for four years on a manslaughter charge that never should've stuck in the first damn place. Surprised the hell out of us that it did. That was when we brought Kevin into the mix, getting rid of the previous lawyer.

Kevin had one job. We paid him a fuck of a lot of money to make Rook his only priority. His single task was to get our brother free, and he needed to get it done sooner rather than later. This was our opportunity for that.

Patience was a virtue. One I didn't fucking have when it came to my club and my brothers. Action needed to be taken.

Judge Hugo White, the judge in Rook's case, didn't like his palms greased. Another problem. But Rook was set to be released in four months and two days from that pit on good behavior, and now the Alabama Department of Corrections wanted to keep him locked up for the full eight years, leaving him four more to serve. That didn't work for me. It definitely didn't work for him.

The change to keep him inside didn't make sense to anyone, but this was something we couldn't control; therefore, Ravage needed to keep tabs on it and be prepared to fight for his release. If we could have controlled this situation, Rook never would have been locked up in the first fucking place. I would've shipped his ass to Mexico or Canada if I'd have known.

"I'll do my damnedest," Kevin said.

Getting straight up in his face not leaving an inch of breathing room, I warned, "Better, because this is your ass if he doesn't get out."

He paled, but nodded and trotted off to his car carrying that stupid briefcase like it had something important in it. Swore he carried it just to use as a weapon if he had too. A lot of good a hunk of leather would do you against a bullet or a crowbar.

Kevin knew what he was signing up for getting involved with us. We'd made it crystal clear before hiring him. He accepted. Therefore, he needed to do his damn job or he'd end up like the previous lawyer. Gone.

Looking up into the sky, it was a sunny, hot day in

Alabama. A perfect day for everything to go to hell it seemed, considering we'd only been home a few hours and this shit landed in my lap.

My cell rang as I made my way into the clubhouse. Ours was different from the Sumner Ravage MC. Theirs was all one floor made of concrete blocks, while ours was not. We had two levels all made of brick and mortar. It was an apartment building at one time, but my father, who was president at the time, had it gutted, redone, and added on to creating a large area with a covered roof for our parties to bleed out onto. He'd even kept the pool, but over the years, it had been dug up and replaced with a much nicer, bigger one. Women loved it and usually ended the night naked inside of it.

Church was held in the basement, and my office was down there next to it. The first floor was the bar, game, and television area. A huge area that we spent most of our time in. The top floor was where most of our club rooms were. It was another upgrade to the building creating a mini apartment for each of us. They were big enough to live in if needed with no problems. A few of the guys wanted to be on the first floor and we made an area in the back for that, but most were upstairs. For us, it worked.

"Crow," I answered, pushing open the steel door to the front of the clubhouse, entering and getting chin lifts from the guys. I returned them, but headed to my office downstairs.

"Hey, Dad." My boy Greer greeted me through the phone as I entered my office, shutting the door behind me.

Falling into the seat that creaked with my weight, my head fell back to rest on the high-backed chair. "Hey."

My office was where most of the Ravage businesses were ran out of. There were stacks of filing cabinets keeping all our documents in place anytime they were asked for. That was the negative of having the motor fuel, liquor and tobacco licenses that covered our outside businesses. Everything had to stay on point.

A large sofa covered one wall with a wide black and white image of the Welcome to Rebellion sign hanging above it. My desk was the original one from my father that he used for more than thirty years. It was part of Ravage history, therefore became my desk as well to continue the legacy.

Three chairs sat in front of the desk, and a bathroom was off to the side only accessible through the room. Behind my desk was a secret room only reachable with keys and a thumbprint on the door. Few had access to it.

"You comin' to my game this week?" Greer asked into the phone. He was sixteen and played on the Panthers high school football team. I went to as many games as possible since he began playing his freshman year, as a starter nonetheless. Now, three years later he was one of the best running backs in the state. He had massive skills on the field, great hand-eye coordination, and fast as hell. Each year he got better and better upping the records from the school by smashing old ones.

There was talk of scouts coming to watch him play, but I wasn't sure that was the path my boy wanted to take. If it was, I'd stand behind him a hundred percent. If it wasn't I'd do the same. If he got a full ride to college with it and wanted to, I'd stand by that as well. If he didn't get a full ride and wanted to go, he'd go. If he wanted to join the club, I'd stand by that too.

The only thing I wouldn't stand for would be him becoming a pussy and not working to earn his way through life. No child of mine would take that road. Therefore, he had some hard decisions coming up in the next year that he really needed to sit back and think about.

He was free to choose his path in life as long as it was something. He would not be thirty-years-old still living with his momma and bumming money off me. Never.

"Yep."

"Right. Can I stay with you after the game?" His tone gave him away, the worry plain and clear about something and it was riding on him hard. My boy felt deeply for those around him with the desire to protect. His mother and sisters were the main focus of this urge. He was still learning how to put that focus and desire into something that he could actually do to solve whatever the problem was, instead of getting angry and going off halfcocked. It was difficult to do when you loved someone, and reigning that in was taking some effort on both of our parts.

He was a kid, though learning his way through life, and this situation could be anything at this point.

"Of course. What's goin' on?"

The phone rustled on the other end. "Can we talk about it when I get there?"

Rubbing my hand down my trimmed beard, I let it go for now. The time to talk would be after the game when I had him face to face and wouldn't let squirm out of talking to me. "Yeah. How's school goin'?"

The line grew quiet for a moment, this telling me he wasn't doing something he was supposed to and his father wouldn't be too happy about it. Usually his grades were pretty good, but lately he'd been having a bit of trouble. "Doin' good."

"Except for?"

He sighed loudly knowing I wouldn't give up. He knew I let go of what he wanted to talk about earlier, and he wouldn't press me on this as well. My boy knew how far to push and two things in one conversation was one too many. "Got a D on my last test in math. That shit is frustrating."

I could only imagine. He brought his math home one day and asked me a question. I went cross-eyed just looking at the problem. Most of the shit they learned now we did the easy way. Schools now did everything the backward, hard way that took thirty minutes to figure out one problem. If I took thirty minutes to figure out one problem in my life, I'd never fucking sleep. He still needed to keep his grades up or no football and no life. "You gettin' help?"

"Yeah. I went to Ms. Airy and she put me with a tutor. I start with her next week."

"Her?"

He chuckled. "Yeah. Her."

I did not chuckle, knowing exactly what I was doing at that age, fooling around and eventually making him. "Keep your dick in your pants, Greer."

"It's not like I'm gonna do her in the library, Dad."

"No, but if she comes over to your mom's house or mine, keep the fuckin' door open. Better yet, study at the table. I do not need to be a damn grandpa."

With humor in his voice, he said, "Not gonna do that to ya. I always wrap up." My patience was beginning to unravel.

"Fuck, boy." This was on a growl. Greer was sexually active, and that shit didn't bother me as long as he was careful. It was the having a kid this young that bothered me. His mother and I had a rough go at it, and I didn't want him to have those challenges. History did not need to repeat itself. That cycle was getting broken come hell or high water. Parents always wanted better for their children. While I couldn't imagine my life without Greer, it was hard having a baby at seventeen.

"Not bringin' home a baby. Chill, Dad."

"Chill? Do not tell me to chill, boy."

He read my *dad* tone. "Really, Dad. It's cool. No kids. Swear it."

"Better not be or I'll tan your ass." Among other things.

"Know that. Gotta split and get to practice."

"Later, boy."

"Later."

Scrubbing a hand over my face, I let all of that go for now. He'd be over Friday night and we could hammer whatever he had going on out. Now, I needed to get club shit done.

WALKING into the convenient store of the gas station, Brewer, Phoenix and Wrong Way behind me, the clerk, Gus, lifted his head as we walked up. "Mr. Crow, how are you doin'?" He was an older man in his sixties and had been working here for three years. Loyal and trustworthy, two very important things when it came to the club.

The club owned several businesses. Some of our very lucrative ones were gas stations with convenient stores attached. We had four in the area. Everyone needed gas, food, smokes, snacks and/or booze and came in droves.

Along with this being a legit money maker, we needed this legal side of the business to cover the other on the not so legal side and be able to make it all work together. And this specific station had a unique purpose, therefore our eyes were on it tight.

Wrong Way, our numbers man, knew what and how to make it all work creating books that were on point each and every time. According to Uncle Sam, we paid our taxes on time and in full. They had no reason to get in our business because we did every-thing to the letter of what they needed. We were keeping it that way.

"Good. You?"

Gus grinned, leaning a hip against the back counter as he looked to each of my brothers lifting his chin in greeting. It wasn't a posture of disobedience or hiding something. It was comfortable, like he should have been born in that very space and the way he took care of it, it could be a strong possibility.

The inside was like any other 'stop 'n rob' in that coolers lined the walls with drinks and booze. Shelves filled the space with snacks and anything else someone on the road would need including car shit, oil, plugs stuff like that. It was good size, but it didn't have hot food because we weren't hiring for that shit, not needing one more government body in our business. We already had permits for the booze, fuel and smokes, we didn't need one more thing.

We had the prerequisite Coke machines and coffee, but other than that, if it wasn't in a bag on the shelf, it wasn't in this store.

Simple. Uncomplicated. Just the way we liked it.

"Good. Need to talk to Carlo. He in the back?"

Gus shook his head. "Nope. Didn't come in today."

Gus' body language didn't change at my tone, but his eyes gave a small flash when I growled, "He do this shit a lot?"

Carlo's ass was supposed to be in this store from seven am to five pm every day except Sunday, no exceptions for holidays. Ravage paid him a shit load of cake for these hours, and him not being here pissed me right the fuck off because from Gus' tone this was a regular thing that we should've known about. Every time we'd come, he'd been here. Right time right place, it seemed.

The man shrugged at me. "Few times a week."

I met Brewer's eyes silently communicating that Carlo just got scratched on the top of our to-do list today. "Right." My voice had a bite as I turned to

Wrong Way. Smart as fuck, except for the one time that earned his name. "Head back and check the books." Everything always came down to the numbers.

He nodded, moving through the aisles.

"Is there a list of shit that needs fixed?" Phoenix asked Gus who nodded reaching under the counter and pulled out a sheet of paper, holding it out in his hand.

"It's not much. Everything's goin' pretty smooth for the most part."

Phoenix took the paper and began reading it as I asked, "For the most part? What's not going smooth?"

Gus shrugged. "Fuckin' sucks when you have to take a piss and you're the only one here."

A chuckle left me. "You gotta piss?"

"Yep."

"Then why the fuck aren't you movin'?"

"Used to holdin' it."

That answer told me exactly how much Carlo was falling down on the job. Gus worked five days a week with Carlo. If he had to control his piss, then this shit had been going on for quite some time.

"Go," I ordered as he met my eyes, released them, then took off to the back.

Turning to Brewer and Phoenix, I demanded, "Get his ass on the phone."

Brewer grabbed his cell and started punching in

the number as I looked to Phoenix and nodded to the paper. "Is it a lot?"

"Nah. A few tiles came up in the women's bathroom, and the Coke machine needs a new hose. It's workin' just needs a new one ordered."

I nodded to him. "Go check it out and get someone on that shit today. Then go check the basement. A speck of fuckin' dust is amiss, I want to know about it."

"You got it," he called out, already on the move. The basement to this property was accessible two ways. One through a hatch in the small building out back where we kept the mower, weed eater, and other shit to maintain the place. One would need to move certain boxes and have a very keen eye in order to find it. It was hidden that well. The other was an underground tunnel that at the end had a large wooden door where we could drive through to get to the basement.

It was very intricate. My father planned it all out and had it executed to the letter.

Since we did business down there, Carlo knew about the space. Not what was in it, but the space, yes. He was a lookout just in case. Therefore, he knew too much.

Looking to Brewer, his head shook as he pulled down his phone, swiped it and began to press a few buttons, and held it up to his ear. After this he said, "Nothing."

"Fucker. You check the place out and make sure it's

good to go. Then help Phoenix. I'm goin' back to look at the books with Wrong Way."

Brewer nodded heading off into the store. Brewer and I grew up together in Ravage. A good, solid man whom I trusted with everything down to the smallest crumb. He was my wing man, always at my back for whatever came our way. We stirred up serious trouble as kids and had minds that thought alike in several aspects. It made us the perfect team to run this club.

Heading back to the small office, Wrong Way was sitting in the chair behind the desk, head down reading the files. I sat my ass in the chair in front of the desk lacing my fingers. "What's the verdict?"

He lifted his head. "The fuckin' verdict is I'm gonna put a fuckin' bullet in Carlo's head."

I leaned forward elbows to knees. "Talk to me."

He turned around the binder, and I peered down at it. The numbers danced over the paper falling into different boxes and categories. The outgoing numbers were flush with the incoming. That shit wasn't right.

"What the fuck?" I asked Wrong Way.

"That's what I want to know. These fuckers weren't like this last month. We had a healthy handle on it. I'm takin' this shit back to the clubhouse so I can compare it with *our* books."

We kept two sets of books on each of our properties. One the government saw, the other only we did, and that one stayed at the clubhouse in the locked room behind my office. But Wrong Way was super efficient and had binders on each property with both sets of books for the past three years.

Before that Leaf ran the books, and those were a clusterfuck. My old man loved the way he did them. I did not and got him out of that job as soon as I took over the gavel. Unfortunately, Leaf passed away a year ago. The diabetes caught up with him.

"Right. I want to know every damn thing that's wrong down to the last fuckin' penny."

"Have a feelin' we'll be takin' that out of Carlo's ass. You get ahold of him?"

I shook my head in the negative. "Nope, but we leave here, he's the first stop. You go ahead to the clubhouse and get this shit organized. Brewer, Phoenix, and I'll take care of him."

"You got it, boss." Wrong Way picked up all the papers for the binder that were turned in all different ways, Carlo sucked at organization, and we walked back out into the store. Gus was back at the register talking to Brewer and Phoenix as I walked up to them. Gus knew nothing of the basement, and it would stay that way.

"We'll get this shit handled." My knuckles rapped once on the glass top where the register lay.

"Got it. I'll be here," Gus replied. He was a good man. Happy at least someone working in this joint was.

Fuck, I was gonna rip Carlo's throat out.

People did not fuck with what was mine. This business was Ravage, and I was Ravage. Therefore, fuck with one, fuck with all, and God save you when that happened. He thought he could pull some sneaky shit... that wasn't going to fucking fly.

Moving out to our bikes, I asked Phoenix, "You get those things handled?"

He reached for his helmet snapping it on under his chin as he swung his leg over his bike. "Yep. Jimmy and Ethan are comin' to fix shit. Basement looks untouched. Opened a few random crates, numbers were spot on."

Jimmy and Ethan were prospects in the club, meaning they weren't patched members, but were working on becoming one. That decision would be a vote with all the brothers in tow and it must be unanimous for anyone to enter.

We were cautious on what jobs they could do, not wanting them to get into the heavy shit until we really knew they were in for the long haul.

Jimmy was our brother Rooster's responsibility. While Ethan was Wrong Way's.

Each prospect had a handler, which was a patched member of the club. The handler's responsibility was to teach their prospect how things worked in the club. If a prospect fucked up, it was on the handler's ass too. It kept everything in line.

The prospects were learning the ropes and earning

their keep. Those two had been solid for the past nine months and proved they could handle fixing up broken shit without their handler present.

"Get Tex, Hornet, and Rooster here to do a full count." Phoenix nodded and made the calls.

After he was done, I called, "Let's roll. Carlo's house."

On a nod, we all three fired up our bikes and took off. The president always took the lead. Brewer on the left and Phoenix on the right at my back as different scenarios of this situation ran through my head. It could be a thousand things.

Carlo was a moron, which was a given at this point. He was stealing from Ravage. Or his mouth was open about what we had going on downstairs. Any of it would end his life.

He lived in a lower to middle class home on the east side of Rebellion. For as much money as we paid him, he could afford better. That was if he didn't have to pay child support and alimony to his ex-wife. Since he did, this place was the best he could do. Not that it was bad, but it was far from luxury.

The ranch-style home was clean cut and well put together. Two houses down from it was not. A total dump with the front door barely hanging on and weeds everywhere. You could tell just from looking who gave a shit and who didn't. Carlo did, but he obviously didn't give one about his job since his Honda

Civic was parked in the small carport off to the left of the house.

At least he was home, making it worth the ride over here. We pulled into the drive, getting looks from some of the neighbors that were sitting out on their porches. It amazed me how many people on this street weren't at work, instead lounging around and getting in others business. Neighborhood watch my ass. More like nosey fuckers.

This meant the three of us kept our eyes moving around us the entire time, not allowing ourselves to be any kind of target. While no one looked like a threat, it could change in the blink of an eye. All it took was one asshole with a bur up their ass. One shot.

While we ruled the town of Rebellion, that didn't mean everyone liked us. Some thought we were what was wrong with our town. Yet, no one ever had the balls to take us on, hell even talk to us. Instead, it was gossip and hearsay behind our backs that we made sure to bring to the light and shut down immediately.

Diligence was just a precaution we took everywhere we went.

Phoenix was the first to knock, putting three healthy raps on the screened storm door. We watched as a car drove slowly down the road obviously taking us in.

"Problem?" I asked Brewer about the car.

"Not yet," he responded as the car moved away.

Nothing at the door.

Phoenix knocked again, this time on the wooden door with his fist making the pounds louder rattling the door, while Brewer went off to the side to see if he could look in the window. He shook his head negative making it back to us. Carlo was locked up tight, but never too tight. There was always a way.

Still nothing.

With a nod to Phoenix, he reached into his back pocket and pulled out his kit with Brewer and I blocking his view from the surrounding homes. Within seconds, he popped the lock moving first into the house with me behind him and Brewer behind me. Phoenix even made a big production of putting his arms up to silently 'greet' Carlo giving the neighbors a good show. Nut. Smart, but still a nut.

There was no one in the walkway or living room. The place was a bit musty and needed the air turned up or the windows opened.

High-pitched moans came from down the hall, though, and that was where we headed. A woman getting fucked. That sound we'd know anywhere. "Fuckin' dick," Phoenix said, moving down the hallway to the noises.

The door was closed, but Phoenix took his boot to it causing it to fly open and crash against the wall, shit flinging off it and crashing to the floor.

Ass in the air, Carlo was pounding into a sexy hot

Hispanic woman, back arched and face wrapped in pleasure.

Upon the crash, he flew off the bed, going to his nightstand and grabbing a gun then pointing it in our direction. Phoenix, Brewer, and I pulled our weapons immediately, and the woman on the bed screeched like a fucking banshee grabbing the sheet and pulling it over her naked body.

"Fuck, guys," Carlo said, lowering the weapon and setting it on his dresser, but we did not. No one pulled guns out on us, unless they knew damn well that they'd better be ready for a bullet to come at them.

"Quiet your bitch down," I ordered as the woman continued the noises, pissing me off. Who the fuck wanted to hear a woman carrying on screaming with no end in sight. Not me that was for sure. She obviously was oblivious to this side of Carlo's world. That was her problem and if she made herself a club problem, we'd really shut her ass up.

"Cool it," Carlo ordered, staring her down.

"What's going on?" She panted, crawling up the bed to the headboard and pulling herself in a ball, the sheet wrapped tight around her.

"Nothin'," Carlos responded and reached for a pair of sweatpants, slipped them on and covered his junk. He'd be lucky I didn't shoot his dick off at this point. We certainly didn't need his seed spreading if he couldn't keep his shit tight. "Can we go into the living room so my woman can dress?" he asked.

"No," I answered, lowering my gun finally, Brewer and Phoenix following, but we kept them at the ready. Always at the ready. A blink of the eye was all it took to bring down a man. "Why the fuck aren't you at work?"

"I wasn't feelin' good."

My eyes flicked to the woman, still wide eyed and breathing hard, but thank Christ keeping her damn mouth shut. "Looks like you recovered."

"Man, I just..."

I took a step closer and Carlo shut his mouth reading exactly what I wanted him to from my demeanor, but I turned to the woman. "Leave." She scrambled wrapping her body in the sheet as she moved, leaving her clothes on the floor and darting past all of us.

Turning back to Carlo, I got in his face and space. "You know too much about our business, Carlo. Know the comings and goings of what we do and how we do it. Knew that comin' into the fold of workin' for us, what would happen if you fucked us over. And yet... you've done it anyway by not showin' up to work."

His olive skin paled and mouth dropped open. "I..."

"No." I swung hard and fast, nailing him in his eye as he fell unceremoniously to the beat up green carpet. Going for the nose would've broken it, and I needed his ass at the store to do his damn job until Wrong Way sorted out what was going on. Not at a hospital getting it fixed. A black eye wouldn't hinder him too much.

Standing over him, Carlo moaned, hand to his eye. "You have fifteen minutes to get your ass to work. You don't show up again, next time you'll see my fists and a bullet. Got me?"

He groaned and said nothing. Therefore, I kicked him hard in the ribs knocking the wind out of him as he rolled and yelped.

"Got me?" I repeated as he nodded, saying some strangled noise that sounded like a yes.

Using my boot, I pushed him to his back and put pressure on his chest. "You got off easy today. There'd better not be a next time. And tell that bitch in there to keep her fuckin' mouth shut."

On that, we turned and left.

At least until we sorted the books and knew for sure what he'd done, he could keep breathing. If Wrong Way found even a fucking dime unaccounted for well, we would revisit Carlo with an entirely different outcome. Until then, he would be smart to get his head back in his business.

Fifteen minutes later, Gus confirmed Carlo was there. He wasn't as dumb as originally thought. Good. You knew it wasn't good when the man who knew nothing was more reliable than the man who did. That shit would be handled and soon.

The next three stores only had minor hiccups.

Carlo was now on all our radars, and one of Ravage would be checking on his ass every damn day.

Just another fucking day at the office. I almost could laugh about it, but alas I had too much shit still to handle; this was just another day in paradise.

If one could call Rebellion, Alabama paradise it would be any brother in the Ravage MC.

4

Rylynn

"I'm surprised you took my call," Nadine said in my ear while I sat on the couch in my apartment. It was small, but exactly right for me.

Giving her a chuckle because she knew I'd never not answer, I replied, "And miss not talking to my Charlie?"

Her laughter came through the line, which I loved hearing. "If only I got paid like Charlie did. I'd be on a jet to Hawaii." She always talked about going to Hawaii. Some of her family was from there, but she'd never been, but wanted to go. I wished I made enough to give her that, but eventually business would grow and maybe one day I could.

"Amen, sister. Whatcha got for me?"

Nadine, Naddy for short, was my Charlie as in Charlie's Angels, in a way in that she took calls and relayed them to me for jobs. Not exactly a receptionist but kind of was. There were two numbers for people to reach me on: mine and hers. It got around by word of mouth. It worked so we rolled with it. Business was steady so we didn't need another avenue.

She sighed and I knew what was coming. That drawn out noise was always a telling sign that I wasn't going to like the jobs, and I was right. "Two different ones. Both cheating men."

My head fell back to the couch. While these were billable hours, it was boring as fuck. Watching men pound away at a side-piece wasn't my cup of tea. Unfortunately, it paid the bills and right now, that's where I was in my career. Everyone had to start some-where, and I wasn't afraid to pay my dues. Sad thing was there were a shit ton of cheating husbands around these parts. Good for me, not so good for the women.

"Anything else?"

"Yes actually." Her tone didn't give anything away, and I could normally read Naddy through her voice. This caught my attention. "A missing person came in."

"What?" This was the very first case that had ever came in, and I'd been doing this since I could drive. Small jobs leading up to bigger ones, but nothing this big. I was still getting my feet wet, but working myself up to hopefully get more well known. This though, was something I wouldn't have expected someone to contact me on.

"Yeah, seventeen-year-old girl. Parents have been looking for her for five months. The cops are at a loss because there are no leads, but the parents aren't giving up. They don't have a lot of money, heard of you through Betty Winger. She was the one with the husband who liked to beat the ass of women before fucking them."

While I remembered the Betty case, my heart hurt for this girl's parents being kept in limbo without a resolution. If it were Mazie, I'd move heaven and earth to find her not caring one bit the cops couldn't find anything. That was where these parents were I'd bet. They wanted answers, and this was the only choice they had in the matter.

None of this sounded good, though. "She's probably dead by now." It was a harsh truth, but it was correct all the same. There was a hard world out there and if this girl got into some of those worlds, she was probably lost. Sad, but I had to say it straight. That was what I did. "If the cops have no leads, the chances of me finding her are slim."

"Know that, but the folks called and I'm relayin'. I'll email you everything on all three cases, and you let me know if you'll take the missing person for sure and I'll give 'em a call."

"Will do. Thanks, Naddy."

"Later, Angel." She laughed, and I felt my lip tip as the call disconnected.

A missing person. I wouldn't lie and say this wasn't interesting. It would beat sitting outside of dingy hotels waiting for a man to meet up with his extra piece. It was more than that, though.

This case drew me in a deep way I couldn't wrap my head around.

I didn't want to say I was excited, because that was fucked up. No one should be excited about a person in the world being lost. For me, it was a challenge. Something I'd loved since I was a kid.

My father would get me these puzzles that were so twisted and hard for me to solve. Sometimes it would take me weeks to figure it out, but I never gave up. Not once, and I got them all. It'd become a tradition for my dad to give me one on my birthday every year. Therefore, I expected a new one in a couple of months.

This though, was a person. A puzzle yes, but a human being.

Five months was a long damn time for someone to be gone and not have any leads. Fuck.

I already knew what my answer would be to Naddy, and she did too. No way would I let this one pass when there was just a hint of me being able to find her.

Dead or alive.

Either one would give the family closure.

Everyone needed that, at least some sort of it.

I'd learned that the hard way with my grandpa dying.

Closure, it was necessary to heal. Knowledge was power and to know this family was literally stuck between living and dying for their child; it was a case I had to take. They probably thought of her every single moment of the day.

There wasn't a single day that went by that I didn't think about my grandpa. The pain still consumed me. It still gnawed at my soul. I was raw in my emotions, my loss. My foothold in life somehow didn't seem so solid anymore.

He wasn't supposed to leave us. His time was too early. He was supposed to be here and watch his grandchildren grow up, see his daughter and her husband through the years, and be next to his wife supporting her as she recuperated.

Instead, he was buried six feet under, in the cold, damp, dark ground.

That single thought alone rattled me.

Part of me wondered if he was in there scraping his nails on the wood of his coffin to get out and come back to us. If he was scared being locked up tight unable to breathe. If he felt captured and out of control because he was a man who needed control and just wanted to breathe again.

It wasn't rational. Deep inside I knew this, but it didn't change the thoughts going on repeat through my head. Each thought made me want to get a shovel and dig him back up, just to make sure his death was real.

Make sure he was really gone and not trying to get back to us.

We'd all said goodbye in the hospital weeks ago. Maybe it was hope. Hope that it was all a dream and somehow I'd wake up seeing the man with the bandana on his head and long braid down his back laughing at the stupid jokes around here.

Except it wasn't.

This was my reality.

Up until now, no one in my life had ever left me in this way. Even with all the members of the club, we'd been lucky. Pops almost left, but didn't. It was a major slap in the face. Or maybe more like a wakeup call.

Life was precious.

The pain of death was hard for those of us who lived. Once the person died they had no feelings. All their pain drifted away once they took their last breath. It was those of us left here to live who felt that agony rip our insides to shreds and had to live with that void in us. In some ways, it was better to be the dead one so you didn't feel this hurt.

Damn my thoughts.

The night we buried him, I buried all the pain in my soul deep inside Crow. Knew I was doing it and didn't give a fuck. Also, knew he'd be leaving and going home. Therefore, in the end, no harm no foul. Was it stupid, yep. Did I plan to never in my life sleep with a brother? Yep. Did my judgment slack and an opportunity presented itself and I took it? Yep. But it is what it is and that part was done. And he was absolutely magnificent, best I'd ever had by a landslide.

Rubbing my hand over my face in exasperation, I rose from the couch. At least in my pain, in my loss, I knew what I was grieving. This girl's family couldn't give up hope when that was all they had left. The pain of the unknown would drive me over the edge. I needed to give them my time, my skill, and help them find the answers they sought. So yup, I was up and facing the tasks ahead rather than wallowing in my grief. There was shit to do today and reliving all of the past wouldn't get me moving.

Walking through my apartment, it was nice having two bedrooms, kitchen, living room and a bathroom. Small, yes, but doable for me. The Ravage MC owned the building, but I paid rent every month. It was a compromise between my father, Rhys, and me.

When I turned eighteen, about two years ago, the decision to move out came naturally. Loved my parents to pieces and would do anything for them, but my father was a hard ass.

Complete tough guy.

Nothing got by him, even to this day he didn't miss details.

Hard ass, through and through.

Being under the thumb of a man who just had to

look at you to scare the living shit out of you was rough.

He'd never hurt me, that wasn't what I meant. A lot of people he wouldn't blink an eye to destroy, but not me. For me, it was the look of when I did something wrong, that disappointment. That killed. Not to mention his punishments were harsh. I missed curfew once, and he made me clean all the toilets and the rest of the bathrooms in the clubhouse. Let's just say, I wasn't late again. Those men were gross.

He loved both my sister and I with everything inside of him, and he'd die to protect us. That I had zero doubt. Me leaving the house wasn't something he was alright with one bit. We fought... a lot. My mother stepped in a few times, but it didn't help much.

It wasn't until I sat my father down and we had a long, calm talk about me and what I wanted out of life and his role in what that would be. He finally agreed for me to move out, under the condition it be a Ravage MC owned place.

My condition was I paid rent. Something else he didn't like. That's what the world was about... compromises. At least with my family.

Family.

I lived for it, loved for it, and became the woman I am because of it.

Two hours later, the words and pictures stared back at me flooding my brain. Naddy ended up having to send it over in a zip file because the parents gave her every single piece of paper the cops had. Didn't know the police did that kind of thing on an open investigation, but they did. From the evidence, the cops were out of options; therefore, I needed to find new ones. A difficult task, but one I was up for.

My phone rang, the display saying, 'Austyn Calling.' One guess as to why she was calling me. I'd been pretty incommunicado the last few days needing to get my head on straight with my grandpa and Crow.

The thing was Austyn watched me leave with him that night with a huge smile on her face as she waved us off. Now, she was going to give me shit and demand all the juicy details of our night.

I answered, "What, Ryker not doin' it for ya? You need a woman to take care of your needs?"

"Smartass." She chuckled. "So how was he?"

"What makes you assume I slept with him?"

She laughed full out, so hard I had to pull the phone away from my ear and could still hear her clearly. "Bitch, if you didn't, I'm revoking your woman card."

"Never wanted the damn thing anyway. It always came with periods," I fired back immediately.

"Those aren't contingent of the card."

"Still don't want it."

"Stop stalling!" She yelled into the line as I chuckled.

"You know I'm not a kiss and tell kind of woman." I rolled off the couch and made it to my kitchen. My stomach needed sustenance. Opening the fridge, the cold air blasted me. Felt damn good.

"Bullshit!" she countered as I rolled my eyes then grabbed a strawberry banana yogurt, shutting the door of the fridge. "Seriously, Ry. Crow is hot. Now I love my man, don't get me wrong, but I'm not blind. The sandy brown hair and bedroom eyes that were locked on you all damn night was sexy. I could feel the intensity of your chemistry across the damn room. Please tell me he knows how to use that hotness."

I opened the container, grabbed a spoon and just took a bite when she said this, and I had to choke down my laughter.

"You're not going to let this go are you?"

"Nope."

Didn't think she would, but it was worth a shot. "He was amazing, Austyn. We had a good time together then he took off for Alabama."

Something inside of me clenched and tightened as I remembered that last kiss. Me standing beside him, him taking what he wanted and giving to me at the same time, the warmth of the machine adding to the heat between us. That spark. It was different than the other guys I'd been with.

It felt real for a moment in time. For him, I could've been anyone from the clubhouse and he wouldn't have cared. I knew how this worked, been around it all my life. There'd been club mommas around every once in a while, and the guys who took them to bed didn't give a shit who it was just as long as it had a warm hole.

What Crow and I did was just that. A way for me to get out my pain and a way for him to get off. There wasn't anything more to it. The clenching inside of me needed to go away because there was no second time. There was nothing but a great night. Two people getting off. That was it.

"Did he give you his number?"

This question solidified it in my head that I was right. "No, Austyn. It was one night. Nothing more."

"You can't tell me that he didn't want more of you, Ry. I don't believe that shit for a minute."

"You been watching me through the window again? You know you could get arrested for that. Wouldn't want daddy Cruz coming to bail your ass out." I shoveled more yogurt in my mouth and listened to her laugh.

"You love it."

Choking down the food, I laughed. "Yeah."

"But seriously. Nothing?" Her tone turned somber and that sucked. She wanted right for me, but picking a guy up at the club wasn't going to be the guy for me. Life didn't work that way. It was the reason I chose him. Knew he'd go away and I wouldn't have to see him with other women every time I stepped through the clubhouse doors. And he was hot.

"It's all good, Austyn. I promise."

"Damn."

Damn was right. One-night stands were just that, no need to relive it or think of it. Life was life. You lived it and moved on.

"Babe. Don't worry about me."

"I'll always worry about you. How are ya doin'?"

About my grandpa, shitty. Heartbroken. Pissed off. "It's hell, but this too shall pass."

"Right. Ryker just left. Something to do with my brother and that chick he likes. Said he wouldn't be back for a few days. So if you need anything call me. I'm around."

"Will do. Later."

We disconnected the call wondering exactly who this chick of Nox's was, but having enough on my plate that my mind needed to keep focused on.

It was time to get busy and make my money. It was also time for the tingling between my legs to go away and for me not to have visions of Crow every freaking moment of the day.

At least one of them, I had control over.

5

Crow

THE DOOR TO THE BACK ALLEY FLEW OPEN, AND TOMMY came to a screeching halt when he saw what was waiting for him. His eyes grew wide then darted around looking for a way to escape knowing he was in deep shit. Too bad for him we always had all our bases covered. There was no way out for him.

Tex, another one of our brothers, walked up to Tommy as he tried to take off in a pitiful attempt and grabbed him by the back of the shirt, tightening it so he couldn't breathe. "And where the fuck do you think you're goin'?" he asked as Tommy's arms flailed trying to pull off the pressure from around his neck, but not getting anywhere.

"Probably to look for his balls," Phoenix joked as he walked closer, each step cracking rocks and glass under his boots. He reached to his buckle and pulled out the large knife he always kept on him, the lights of the building sparkling off the blade.

Phoenix had a thing with knives. If one were to check his body, they'd be surprised to find at least ten if not more on him, at all times. While he used his gun, knives were his specialty, choosing them above all other weapons. He put the sharp blade to Tommy's throat.

"Nah, he never had those in the first place," Rooster, another brother, commented, coming over to stand next to me and Brewer, who both had our guns out.

"We gave you ten grand," I started, crossing my arms over my chest and taking a menacing step forward. "You haven't made that ten K and left us hangin'. Then *we* had to come find *you*. We don't go huntin' for shit we pay for. So Phoenix here is gonna take it out of your skin."

Tommy coughed and squirmed, face turning red, but Phoenix didn't even blink pressing the blade into Tommy's throat harder and causing a bit of blood to run down his neck. Not enough, but it would serve the purpose.

"I have it." The words came out broken and wheezing, which would be expected.

The source who connected us with Tommy said he was a piece of shit, but gave reliable information. Since we trusted the source, we were putting that on Tommy.

If this shit went south, there'd be two more deaths on my hands very soon. Carlo and Tommy.

Tex lessened the pressure around his neck as Tommy gasped for breath.

"Oh, you do? Then why are ya runnin' from us?" I said, calm and cool watching his facial expressions and body movements, getting a read on him, which was difficult with him trying to suck air in his lungs. "What do you have for us?"

Phoenix stepped back a touch as Brewer kicked Tommy's feet out from under him having him land hard on his ass to the dirt-covered ground. He cried out, and Tex grabbed his shirt keeping him in place.

"I'm waiting."

Tommy's eyes flickered everywhere, no doubt trying to come up with some kind of information that he would hope would pass. This made me curious as to what all he knew, and whatever he gave us would decide his fate. Tommy was a weasel, but one with connections around this city. He was vapor, never seen unless he wanted to be. This afforded him to be very knowledgeable.

Nodding at Tex, he released his grip on the t-shirt and Tommy swayed putting his hands around his neck protectively. He looked up to me from the ground knowing his time was going to be up if he didn't give me something tangible that we could run with to get more information. We paid him to get his ass moving fast, that was obviously a mistake, but I wanted my ten grand of information.

No one fucked with the Ravage MC, and Tommy knew it but signed up for the job anyway. This would decide how stupid he was going to play it.

"Xavier and Marcus. Low level in the drug department, but moving up the ranks. Rumor is they are planning on taking up with Dixon in Midway to get bigger shipments. Their distribution is spreading, but it hasn't gotten anywhere close to Rebellion."

"It better fuckin' not," grumbled Phoenix.

He wasn't fucking kidding there. Xavier Glenn and Marcus Camery contacted us to do a run for them. We were to pick it up on the Chattanooga by boat, then meet them at a warehouse to drop off the goods. We did not ask specifically what was in the crates, but were getting a pretty good idea now.

"They have a small crew, but they're all loyal to Xavier and Marcus."

He said nothing, just stared up at me. He had to have more here. I reached in and pulled out my Glock, holding it to my side. "We're not exactly gettin' ten grand worth that we paid for."

Phoenix sunk the knife into Tommy's thigh causing him to cry out in pain once again. Blood trickled down splashing to the concrete and mingling with the filth already there. At closer look, the wound was only a flesh. Phoenix barely cut him. Pussy.

Tommy's breathing was labored. "Fuck!"

Kneeling down to look him in the eye gun at the ready, I responded, "You'd better fuckin' talk."

"Shit!" he ground out as I moved my gun to the knife wound, pushing it down into his flesh and causing more of his blood to spill. Tommy hollered out again in pain as I ground the gun into his leg.

"Better get talking. My finger's gettin' twitchy."

He heaved in a breath after I let up the pressure, fear stark in his eyes. "This doesn't have anything to do with Marcus and Xavier, but word on the street is you have eyes on you."

"What the fuck?" Brewer growled at my side, looking down at us. He wasn't wrong. Eyes were bad. Eyes got us in deep shit.

"Don't know who yet. Whoever they were they're keeping a tight hold on it. Even I haven't been able to find out who."

Pissed off I shot a round in Tommy's thigh then rose to my feet, and my brothers closed in. Spent my life counting on my gut and this asshole had nothing more to give us, at least at the moment he was telling the truth. Fuck, we had a target on our backs.

The ten grand wasn't a complete loss, but he was nowhere near done yet. He needed to get digging and fast.

"Get me my ten grand worth. I want to know who the eyes are. You have two days to get me more information or you won't be breathin'," I said looking down at Tommy. "Let's roll," I ordered as Tex let the man go, and he fell to the ground with a thump. Phoenix put his knife back in its holster, and I put my gun away.

Walking back to our bikes, I stopped Wrong Way. "Get your fuckin' brother on the phone and to the clubhouse." He nodded, pulling out his phone and making a call. Maybe Kenny knew something. He was the sheriff of Rebellion and all.

We got on our bikes and rode back to the clubhouse. Me at the front, Brewer and Wrong Way behind me, behind them Rooster, Hornet, Lemon and Tex. We were one. Loved riding with my brothers, but my head was on to this new situation.

For the last few years, we'd flown under the radar never pinging on anything. When I became president, I took great pains to make that happen. Loved my dad, but some of his dealings were a bit sticky and got us in some heat. Instead of keeping that on us, the club moved in another direction where we were more discreet about what we did.

Everything appeared legal to anyone looking at us. Therefore, no shit thrown our way. This, though. Having someone watching us, that could only lead to bad things and needed to be stopped immediately.

Kenny should know if it had anything to do with the law, such as ATF which if it was, we'd be fucked if they went in and found our stashes. The goal was always to be miles ahead of anything and everything. Unfortunately, this made us lag behind. We needed to get a tight handle on it and get it controlled.

Pulling into the clubhouse, we parked our bikes, swung off them, and took our helmets off.

"What are you thinkin'?" Texas, or Tex for short, asked as the hot sun pounded down on us. Tex had been in the club for over twenty-one years and was a mountain of a man at six-two and built like a solid tank.

"Inside," I ordered as we all went into the clubhouse and down to church. Lemon shut the door. Our church room was large and had concrete walls all around it from every angle. Since it was in the basement two of those walls were a given, but we put in two more to make it extra secure.

Large cherry doors opened wide inside and shut tight to keep everything in the clubhouse secret. There were a lot of those in the club.

When I became president, the table in the center of the room changed. In the beginning, it was a round, solid cherry wood table with the Ravage insignia of a skull with flames coming out of its head in the center with the name Ravage carved into it.

Six of us. Brewer, Wrong Way, Hornet, Rooster, Tex and I redid the table. We didn't touch the original one, keeping all the dents and scratches from years of churches visible. We used the round table as a guide, made a large rectangle and fit it around the original table so it was centered in the middle of it. The outer wood was lighter and varnished making the round one stand out.

It was large enough to handle our brothers. The new dents and scratches only added to the personality of the piece.

It was a club vote to change the table, because it wasn't large enough for all of us, but no way would we lose the original.

"Check the room," I ordered as my brothers looked at me. "We don't have a fuckin' clue who this could be, so check the fuckin' room and make sure it's not bugged."

On a nod, we all scattered around the room, searching. Everything could be done wireless these days, making the task of identifying cameras more difficult.

"Clear," was called out several times. While I didn't think any part of the club was bugged, we'd be checking all of it to make sure.

"Sit," I ordered, taking my seat at the head of the table. Brewer next to me on one side while Wrong Way was on the other. "Anyone get any indications they were being watched?" The guys instincts were good having that gut that could tell when something was amiss.

While they would've brought it to me as soon as they felt it, I had to ask.

"No," came from several around the table.

Wrong Way spoke, "We've got camera on all the stores, stations, and buildings. Goin' through it all will take time, but if Hornet's good with it, Jimmy can start looking through them. Lemon just needs to get them up for Jimmy."

Lemon was our tech man. He had a lot of skills when it came to computers, yet he was learning how to hack sophisticated systems still. Not quite there yet, but he had promise considering he kept all the shit he was doing under wraps. He'd only been a patched member for three years, the same time I'd been president. He said, "On it," got up from the table and went down the hallway, no doubt to his room where his computers were.

He had a room with a bank of screens and several keyboards. How he kept all that shit straight I didn't know and didn't care as long as it was done.

Everything these days was on those damn electronic things, and if Lemon didn't get his shit together and be able to hack the right places, we'd have to find someone who did. Finding ears and eyes outside the club wasn't something we were willing to do. Lemon had better pull through.

Hornet and Rooster rose as one as usual. Those two

were stuck together tight all the time. One didn't go without the other. Anywhere. "We'll start searching the clubhouse in and out for any eyes or microphones. We have the bug sweep. We'll do the entire property," Hornet told the group, throwing out his help. It was the main reason I wanted to become the president of this club. Family. Each of us putting in our bit to help to solve the problems. All of us working together to protect our own.

"Do we have extra bug sweeps?" I asked Hornet.

"Think we have three," he replied.

That wasn't very many at all for the job we were going to need to accomplish. I looked down to the end of the table where Bear sat. He was older than my father and had been around since the beginning of the club. He didn't do much of the *grunt work* as he called it, but we needed him.

"Bear. Need you to find three more bug sweeps. Out of town with cash."

He nodded. "That I can do."

"Thanks. He gets back get everyone on the bugs, room by fuckin' room. You go to the stores and cut the feed first, then sweep. All hands on deck for this. Go," I ordered, watching Hornet, Rooster, and Bear leave out the church door.

I turned to Wrong Way. "First, what did ya find with the store?"

"Still workin' on that."

"Alright, after that make sure all the paperwork for

each of our properties is in the holding companies name and not ours. Know it is, but just want you to double check that one didn't slip through the cracks. The rental houses, the gas stations, licenses—everything. Don't know who this fucker is and want everything as clean as possible."

"Lucky for me I keep up that shit regularly. It'll be done in an hour then I'll get back to the books at the store." Wrong Way was our secretary. He kept all the documents and numbers going in the right direction. He was so fucking organized he put that Martha Stewart bitch to shame. There was no doubt having to redo all the books that Carlo did was pissing him off more than it was me, which said a lot.

"And make sure the girls are taken care of."

He smiled at this. "That is not a problem."

"The minute your brother gets here, I want him in my office," I told Wrong Way, who nodded and took off.

Looking around the room, I commanded, "See what everyone needs help with and fill in. Priority one is the bug sweep. Then if you're free, start at the stores then go to the warehouses."

"On it, bossman." More guys filtered out of the room leaving Brewer and me sitting alone at the table. He and I had a bond for years, and when my dad wanted to step down as president and put me in his spot, Brewer had to be my number two. He was smart, forward thinking, a listener and kick ass brother.

"What are ya thinkin'? he asked after scoping out the room once more. He was a very cautious man, another admirable trait.

"I'm thinkin' we're gonna get fucked up the ass if we don't reign this in and now." Wiping my thumb over my bottom lip in thought, I turned to my second-in-command. "Whoever this is we decapitate them."

"On it."

Fuck, we needed to figure out who or what this was. Protect the club, always.

* * *

"KENNY, what do ya got for us?" I asked him, leaning my ass into my desk with Wrong Way sitting in front of me in one chair and Kenny in the other. Kenny leaned back in the chair casual as could be.

"There's nothin' on my end, Crow."

"You're sure?" I asked, crossing my arms over my chest. Kenny was a good man. He upheld the law in Rebellion and looked the other way when it came to Ravage. In return, we kept our city clean from the trash that had threatened to make its way inside the city limits. It was a relationship that worked out well.

Therefore, he was telling us the truth putting a huge dead end sign on that lead.

"Thanks, you hear anything you call your brother."

"You got it." Wrong Way took Kenny out of my office and Brewer walked in.

I shook my head. "He doesn't know anything. We may need to call in Warden."

Brewer sucked in his bottom lip. "You think he'd come back?"

"He'd better, he still has that patch on his back."

"Right," Brewer said. "I'll make some calls and see if I can find him."

"Do that." I slapped him on the back as we made our way up the stairs and into the main area of the clubhouse. Grabbing a beer from the cooler, I sat at the bar hating the idea that this could be anyone. I trusted my brothers with everything. The prospects were earning it, but there was always that possibility and as much as I hated to think it, I needed to open my eyes to that possibility.

The clubhouse door swung open and in walked a very leggy brunette, hand over her nose, blood pouring out of it. Fuck.

"Tex!"

Brewer went up to the woman, Stephanie, and wrapped his arm around her waist, sitting her down on a chair by the bar.

Stephanie had tears rolling down her face, smearing her mascara as it mixed in with the blood.

"What the fuck happened?" I bellowed, and she stiffened as Brewer gave her a towel to put on her nose and tilted her head back. Stephanie's eyes were already starting to bruise underneath, and it would only get worse.

"My guy tonight. I gave him what he wanted. Then he punched me, took the money back, and left," she said through a nasally nose.

"What the fuck?" Tex joined the mix. He was in charge of our stable of thirty-five women. We didn't pay for pussy, but others sure did. The girls paid us twenty-five percent of what they made for protection and the use of the Ravage name for that purpose, which normally held a weight that no one would fuck with the girl.

This shit, though. This didn't happen. This wouldn't fucking happen. Not on my watch.

"Steph, who the fuck was it?" Tex asked, kneeling down before her. One thing Tex had was a love for the ladies and a fierce urge to protect them. All in all, it worked out well.

"Blake Graden, at least that's the name Goldilocks gave me. He made me call him 'B'." Goldilocks took care of the booking and vetting of the men wanting to spend time with the women. She was also Bear's ol' lady and a fierce lioness. She gets one look at Stephanie and heads would roll.

Tex pulled out his phone, tapped on the pad, and put it up to his ear. "Did you vet a Blake Graden?"

"Right, well Steph is here with a busted nose." Tex

held the phone away from his ear, the sounds of Goldilocks screaming filling the room. Pissed. That was why she was perfect for this job.

"Goldi!" Tex bellowed in the line. "Need you to pull up everything you have on him and email it to me in the next ten minutes. I'm going to call the doc and get his ass here to set her nose. After the info, need you here for her."

"Right." He swiped the phone off.

"I'll take care of this, Crow."

"Know you will. Want to know what's goin' on. And then we're payin' a visit to Blake."

He nodded once, then got on the phone calling the doctor, a guy we paid under the table, then going back to Stephanie.

Brewer came up beside me. "After Tex gets the info, call me. We're spread thin, but this is a priority."

"Got it," Brewer responded quickly.

"This fucker will pay."

He would, the Ravage way.

6

Rylynn

PRESSING THE BUTTON ON THE CAMERA REPEATEDLY, asshole husband case two was indeed cheating on his wife and something told me she wouldn't be too keen on seeing the pictures currently on my memory card. Her husband was wearing a pony head with leather straps all over his body criss-crossing this way and that, and he was pretty ripped; definitely spent time at the gym. The guy behind him had the leather reins attached to the husband's mouth in his hands, using the force to fuck married man hard in the ass.

Too each their own. While I didn't get off on pony play, this guy obviously did and didn't want his wife to know. Or hell, maybe she did know and wouldn't participate with him. Every relationship was different between people.

There was no textbook right or wrong because

everyone had unique likes. It was finding that person in the world who had those same likes as you and fitting together like a puzzle piece. It wasn't an easy task. Most of the time we had to go through a hell of a lot of duds to hopefully come out on the other end with someone who fit.

Other times, some never found their fit and were left alone. While others were completely content on being alone and didn't want to deal with a partner on a daily basis.

Each person, life, choice and love was different.

In this case, from the paperwork I read from the wife, she was going to have a coronary considering she taught Sunday Bible school and didn't know where her husband 'lost his way from Jesus.' Seemed she only *thought* she knew her husband.

Knowing that I'd need to do this a few more times to establish a pattern instead of a one-time thing, I climbed down from the bucket I stood on and looked into the dingy motel room. Yes, it was a motel in every sense of the word. It'd seen better days about thirty years ago and was just getting worse.

Heading to my Jeep, I tossed the bucket in the backseat and set the camera down on the floorboard after quickly checking the shots, fired up, then got the hell out of there.

The case on the missing girl had a lot of moving parts, and just reading through all the reports and evidence was a bit overwhelming, but doable. It needed to be processed in the way my brain could sort it all out.

While I was still reading and brainstorming on that case, the cheating husbands were easier to get done so I bumped them up on the priority list to get them out of the way so I could focus on the missing girl. Considering they didn't fuck their playthings all the time, it gave me time to think about Elizabeth, the missing girl.

My phone rang from my back pocket. I lifted, pulled it out, and looked at the display which said 'Mazie Calling'. Answering, I greeted, "What's up, monkey?"

"Dad won't let me go to Payton's house."

A smile tipped my lips. "And what? You called me to change his mind? Because you do know I have the magical powers from the unicorns to do that."

"You can. He listens to you."

I laughed full out as I pulled into traffic. Even at ten-years-old she got my sarcasm. It was quite impressive. "No, monkey. He doesn't."

"When you wanted your bike, Dad let you."

This was going to be a battle, I could already tell, and it wiped the humor out of the situation. My baby sister, who was ten going on thirty, thought she could do whatever she wanted whenever she wanted. With our dad being overprotective and only now having one child under his roof, I was sure it was ten times worse.

Add in him just losing his best friend, my grandpa, and I was sure Dad had Mazie locked up like Fort Knox. Still, there were certain things where Mazie had him in the palm of her hand. This was not one of those things.

"Maz, that bike was very old. Dad and I worked together to restore it. Hours we spent, Maz. That's why he didn't say anything. He appreciates it when you work hard."

"What about you leavin' here?!" she yell-screamed in my ear, forcing me to hold the phone back a foot. "He let you move out!"

Mazie had a lot to learn about life. She'd been around everyone at the Ravage MC for so long that she thought she walked on water because everyone thought she was adorable and everyone catered to her. Mom and Dad allowed this, but if they didn't pull her ass back and soon, she was going to turn into a little shit and that was fast approaching. No way my sister was going to be the shit kid. I knew our parents were over compensating for me leaving and Grandpa dying and weren't in the right mindset for this now. Therefore, it was up to me to do so.

"You need to ride this out, Maz. You're ten. You have eight more years before you even think of having a say-so in your life. No use in getting angry because it won't change anything."

"I know. Just sucks." She sounded defeated on the other line, which was better than fired up to take on

Dad, the man she'd never take down once he made up his mind, attitude she threw around since getting on the phone.

"It does, Maz. Gotta give Mom and Dad this time."

"They're really sad about Grandpa." She sniffled, and I wished I was there to wrap her in my arms.

She was so damn young to lose someone so close to her. I hated that for her, but there was nothing that could be done at this point. She was my little sister, and I wanted to shield her from all life's pains. But what I had learned from losing my grandfather was losing hurt, living hurt, and feeling that all was agony.

Time. That was what all of us needed now and when you needed it, it dragged on feeling like it would stay in the vicious cycle forever.

"They are, and you need to give them a break. Let them deal with their loss the way they need to."

"I miss him." Her voice broke, and I pulled off to the side of the road feeling my chest tighten.

"I know you do, monkey. We all do."

Some days, moments like this, I wondered if the pain could swallow us all whole. Make us go down the rabbit hole of grief to the point of not coming up. Our family was strong, my father made sure of that. But with this, could we remain that way? If one fell, it would be like a deck of cards, each of us going after.

"Why does stuff like this have to happen, Ry? Why

can't people just live and be happy? Why do they have to die?"

The emotion coursing through me clogged in my throat. The pain my family was feeling, I couldn't take away. There was no way to 'make them feel better,' because there was no better at this point.

Grandpa was gone, and there was never a chance to change that fact. There was only coping, learning how to carry on. That was all we could do. Our choices were taken away from us.

"It just does, Maz. Life is life, and you can't change things that have happened already. You have to figure out ways to deal with the changes. It won't be right away, but it will happen."

"It doesn't feel like it."

"I know. It won't for a while. Just chill for a bit and everything should go back to normal." At least I hoped, but the truth was nothing would ever be *the* normal we had before Grandpa died. It would now be a new normal that we'd all have to adapt to. It would be hard on everyone, but Mazie would get the brunt of the overprotectiveness because it was something my mother and father could control.

After losing your control, people did anything to get it back. It was like a cancer patient. They had no control over what was growing inside of them. When they started chemo, those toxins did something to the body that made them lose their hair. Some people chose to cut it off before it all fell out. While others waited. It was a control that they had some grasp on and made the decision to do. Each person having a different view on it, but it was theirs. It was the only control over what was happening to their bodies.

It was the same situation when you lose someone you love. You grasped at anything you could trying to hold on to the tangible things, thinking at any moment all of it could be swiped away from you. It was a fear that everything could change in the blink of an eye. Mazie was just caught in the crossfire.

"Okay. I have to go. I have math homework," she said with the ease of Mazie, the girl she was.

Like our father, she was tough. The good thing with kids, they had the ability to push shit aside and move on at least for a moment. She could still ignore the emotions in the depths of her heart and soul.

"Get it done, monkey."

"Bye."

"Later." Hanging up the phone, I pulled back out in traffic. My dad could have a number of reasons for not allowing my sister to go somewhere, and I wasn't stepping on any of that. Certain things were worth standing up for with him. Not going to a friend's house was not one of them. There were bigger fish to fry in life, and Mazie needed to learn that.

Looking at the clock on the dash, I realized I was

late. Gunning the Jeep, I made it to the gym with a minute to spare. Rylie was still going to kick my ass.

Deke's ol' lady had been training me for a while now, and she made me pay for it dearly when I was late. Excuses didn't work on her.

Ever.

It was what I loved about her. No bullshit. We needed more people like her in the world.

Except now, my body was going to get ran over by a truck and slammed with a hammer. I'd for sure need ice tonight.

As the saying went, what doesn't kill us only made us stronger... that would be my workout.

7

Crow

"WHAT THE FUCK, GOLDI?" GOLDILOCKS' BROWS WERE knit in anger as she surveyed Stephanie's face. The doctor came to the clubhouse and did his thing. Steph was now packed with gauze with a reset nose and on serious painkillers about to pass out asleep. It was the best thing for her at this point.

She wasn't one who could handle a blow like that. Instead, she was more likely to pet kitties at a shelter, find a nine to five husband, give him twelve kids and dinner on the table when he got home. Why she chose this life, I didn't know. Her body, her choice.

Ravage was not a pimp show. We did not ever cross those lines. Goldi would check out the guys the girls wanted to hook up with and collect our twenty-five percent. Ravage didn't get involved unless a situation like this arose.

We only offered protection, and our load was getting larger. Tex was dealing with that and keeping it at a reasonable number, but the women heard from others about how we did things in Rebellion. They then came to us wanting the same thing.

Hooking wasn't a glamorous job, but when bills need to be paid, they did what they had to do. We just wanted them to do it safely.

Of course, it was against the law for women to be ladies of the night. Therefore, the money was cash to us always, keeping us in the clear. It also helped that we had Kenny who looked the other way knowing that we were protecting the women. It was one of the many things we tight-roped on, and fuck if that was going to come crashing down on us.

"Everything on him checked out. Name, address, job. Everything."

"Not fuckin' everything," Tex growled, running his hands through his hair, frustration riding him hard. He was ready to attack. No one fucked with his girls.

Goldi put her hand to her cocked hip. "You think I'd put my girls in that spot?"

"No. Let's take a ride," Tex said, putting an arm around Goldi and kissing the top of her head. He knew like everyone else in the club that Goldi would kill the fucker for even thinking it.

She was a solid woman. The best. It was why she had the job she did.

TEX HELD out his arm pointing to the house in question. It was the affluent part of Rebellion with large homes, yards kept, and everything pristine. The windows had sheer curtains on them, and movement could be seen on the inside.

We looped around and pulled into the driveway, cutting the engines and going to the door. Tex knocked and a few moments later the door opened as a short, rounded brunette whose eyes widened at the sight of us answered. We had that effect. We were large and intimidating to most. Good thing we had some of the guys stay at the clubhouse to continue the search for bugs. This woman would've shit her pants with us all and ran in the house like a scared mouse.

"We're here to see Blake," Tex said on a friendly smile. That fucking smile served him well. It could mean he was going to tear your heart out or he liked you. It just depended on his mood. He said he learned it from watching me. What-the-fuck-ever.

"There's no Blake who lives here," the woman said hesitantly, fear glittering in her eyes that kept darting between the three of us. Her hand on the door started to slightly tremble. "What's going on?"

"Just need to talk to Blake Graden." Tex went for it again not giving up. Ravage never gave up.

Her hand on the door tightened turning her knuckles

white, and she was about to give us the same spiel again so I cut in. Nice wasn't cutting it so we needed to go in hard.

"Ma'am, do you know who Blake Graden is?"

She shook her head.

"What is your husband's name?" She had a wedding ring on therefore I thought it pertinent to ask.

"Berry."

Tex looked over to me thinking the same thing. The dickhead who hurt Steph made her call him B instead. Chances were, this was the fucker.

"Where is he?"

She shook her head, her hair flowing with the movement. "I don't know."

"Don't lie to us," Tex growled, making the woman jump back a foot, eyes terrified, and I swore I could see her heart pounding hard through her shirt. She was a scared little rabbit not wanting to get eaten.

"I'm not. He left our kids and me a while ago. He hasn't even called, and he for certain hasn't paid any of our bills."

The way she trembled this time, she was telling the truth. She may be scared, but she was also one pissed off woman who got hung up at the toes.

Tex pulled out a business card and handed it to her. "If he calls or comes home, I need you to call me. Can you do that?"

"Will you hurt him?" Her eyes darted back and

forth between all of us. While trying to get a read on it, I couldn't tell if she wanted us to beat the shit out of him or if she was really concerned that we would.

"No, just wanna talk," I lied, and the way her shoulders drooped just a touch told me she bought it or was sad. Yeah, this woman knew nothing of the underworld. One where her husband more than likely played. I felt the need to punch him just for putting that look on her face.

She took the card. "Okay."

Nodding, we took off, walking to our bikes.

"You think she knows?" Tex asked low even though the woman threw the door closed.

"We're gonna find out. Find a time when that car isn't in the driveway, and we'll go in and scope it. Need to do this asap. You think Wrong Way's prospect Ethan is ready for this shit?"

Tex nodded. "He's comin' into his own. It's time to get him involved with this shit."

"Good."

I moved to Wrong Way. "You think your guy could handle a stakeout?"

"Yep."

"Good, call him. Get him in a car parked outside this house out of sight. He calls when the woman leaves, and we go in quiet."

Wrong Way nodded, pulling out his phone and

making the call. When that was done we got on our bikes and rode out, headed back to the clubhouse.

We all worked as a team, each man having some part in our operation to be in charge of. It was like a corporation, and I had CEOs underneath me. Not that I'd ever see any of these fuckers in a suit. That thought made me smile. It worked well for us over the years. No reason to change something that wasn't broken.

———

"UPDATE." Brewer came up to me while I sat in the bar area of the club sucking a beer as I ran scenarios in my mind. The prospect hadn't called so it didn't look like we were gettin' in the house tonight. If she didn't get out in the morning, I'd come up with a way to make it happen.

Waiting was none of our strong suits. We liked shit done and fast.

"Yeah."

Brewer started. "First, no bugs detected anywhere in the clubhouse. Lemon is tracking to see if they cut into our feed, but said his system is unbreakable."

"Right. Just like his hacking skills. That's good news. What about the stores?"

"Two found at the main location. One by the front door and one inside. The size of a fuckin' dime. It was the only one that had them."

"You think whoever this is knows about the shit in the basement?"

He nodded. "That'd be my guess."

"Fuck." I ran my hand over my face. "We'll need to move the shit."

Brewer's face twisted. "Yeah, but where?"

"Get on the phone and see if you can find buyers. That way we can unload it and not worry about it for now. Give us time to get down to the bottom of what's going on."

"I'll call. There's more."

"Christ," I bit out.

"Info on Blake. He does work at Cannoin Industries as stated in the report, but he's not our guy."

I took a swig. "How do you know this?"

"He died a year ago."

I leaned back in the chair plopping the bottle on the table. "Fuck. That's why everything else checked out too." Fucker used a dead man's information to get through to Stephanie.

"Yep. Need to make sure Goldi is checkin' shit deeper. The first thing from now on she looks in the fuckin' obituaries."

"Talk to Bear about it. He'll get her straight."

"Right. Next, Berry Alabaster, the woman's husband is ghost. No credit cards used, checks written, or bank withdrawals for the past four months. He's made no electronic connection to his wife or anyone at all. No Internet footprint whatsoever. Like he's vapor."

"Ghost or not. We find him. Find Tommy and impress on him that this is part of our ten grand. Two people for him to find."

He rapped his knuckles on the table. "On it and I'll get Lemon to dig deeper on Barry."

"Good."

Brewer took off, and I let everything happening around me process, running through the different scenarios, trying to fit the non-existent puzzle pieces together. My brain was a damn storage closet flinging papers out of it left and right. The only times I'd gotten it to calm down was on my bike and with Rylynn.

A delicate hand grazed over my shoulders and Carley came around in front of me. "Hey, Crow," she cooed. Carley was one of the club girls who spent her time with a majority of us. She wasn't in the stable. She gave it free and willingly all the time. With long curly hair, pretty eyes, and a nice body, she got her fair share of playtime here.

"Hey. How's it goin'?"

She slid down to her knees in front of me, her head in line with my cock. Her hands caressed my thighs to my knees, her eyes begging and greedy. My cock twitched. I hadn't gotten off since I left Rylynn back in Sumner. We never got to the point where I had her on her knees in front of me. Fuck, just picturing her like that had my cock hardening and lengthening. Rylynn's face lighting up as she licked the crown of my dick.

With my cock between Ry's lips, she wouldn't have had a chance to use that smartass mouth since I'd stick my cock all the way down her throat and get her to make some more of those sexy sounds she did when I fucked her.

Carley took my erection as her invitation and unbuttoned my jeans, pulling my cock out and slipping it between her lips as a groan escaped. Her mouth was hot and wet as she began to suck me off in earnest, putting me all the way down her throat. When I looked down at Carley though, I didn't see her.

Instead, I saw blonde silky hair that had fallen down like a sheet and the greenest eyes that reminded me of grass in the spring. Rylynn was kneeling before me, her mouth sucking me off. Her eyes burning with lust and desire. Her wanting to do everything to please me. Fuck.

It felt damn good, and I closed my eyes letting the visions of Rylynn naked and under me fill my thoughts. The way her tight body arched when I slipped my cock inside of her. Her noises when I thrust deep in her wet pussy. Her nails scratching the hell out of my back, adding a bit of pain to the pleasure. All of it wound around me tight.

My hand went to the woman's head as my balls drew up and hot come expelled from my cock. The hair didn't feel right between my fingers though, and when I looked back down, Carley was sitting there eyes on me and licking my cock clean. Pulling my hand away, it felt as though it was covered in acid.

Never had this been a problem before. Never had I had any other feelings during head except to get off and do it hard. This time felt different, not right. It wasn't the woman looking up at me who I wanted to be there. It wasn't her face filled with want who needed to be on her knees in front of me that I craved.

It weakened the intensity of the orgasm to something that wasn't even worth my time, and what man would ever say that shit? A guy came. It felt good. Done. Normally. This time it felt unsatisfying to say the least.

I pulled away from her scooting my chair with me, standing up and zipping my pants. Carley looked up at me expectantly wanting to get hers too, but that wasn't going to happen. She wasn't the one I wanted to sink into. It didn't even appeal to me one bit.

"Thanks."

Disappointment flooded her face, but I didn't give a fuck. She did her job here at the club, and in return the Rebellions give her a safe haven place to stay. It worked, and she'd need to get the fuck over it.

Leaving her on the floor, I made my way to the TV room where my dad was sitting in one of the recliners. I slapped him on the shoulder. "Hey. How are ya?"

He looked up at me, his face showing his age and experience. His skin had turned leathery over the years —all that time out in the sun on his bike riding. The gray goatee and hair helped that along as well. Years he'd been the president of the club, but about four years ago he decided it was time to call it quits and he started grooming me for the position. A year later I took over and hadn't ever looked back. I'd been a member of the club since I was eighteen. There was nothing else I wanted to do but be part of this club. Even before that, I grew up here. Learned here. This was home.

My father had been my rock my entire life and still was to this day. If ever a man deserved respect, it was him.

"Good, son. Thought I'd come see the game." His head nodded to the television as I plopped into the seat next to him. My father would always be a member of the Ravage MC, but he'd pulled back in the past couple of years because his health hadn't been the greatest.

"I'd have come in earlier if I'd have known you were here."

His hand clasped my forearm giving it a small shake. "You're a busy man. Believe me, I understand."

He would and was probably the only person I could talk to about all the shit on my shoulders. It wasn't the time for it.

"Talk to me." The order came out just as such to my father. Loved the old man, but he went to the doctor yesterday and didn't call me. Not that I expected him to, the stubborn old man. He was one of the very few on this planet that I wouldn't shoot in the head for not following orders.

The man was as headstrong as they came and took zero shit, which he passed on to me. Times like these though, I could strangle him.

"The treatment is working."

This shocked the shit out of me so much I grabbed the remote, turned off the television, and got in my dad's space. "Really?"

His smile was forced, not giving me a good feeling. "Yes, son. Really." My father was diagnosed with prostate cancer two years ago and had been going through chemo and radiation. Both not getting all the cells out. There was an experimental drug that the doctors said would be good for him. I pushed him to do it. He did, eventually.

"So it's killing the bad cells and your body is producing good ones?"

His eyes were warm as he looked at me. This time the smile was genuine, and I felt the knot in my chest subside. "Yes. Things are going well."

"Is Kara taking you to all your appointments on time?"

His smile widened. "Oh, Kara is taking care of your old man just fine."

I sat back in the chair and grabbed the remote. The little tingles in the back of my neck told me something was off. My father wouldn't lie to me unless it was something big, and that something would be that the medicine didn't work and he was trying to save me from knowing this information. But he looked me in the eye, so for now I believed him. He knew I'd be pissed as hell if he lied.

"You need more help, old man? Got lots of women who'd love to give ya a hand."

He chuckled. "Back in the day I'd say fuck yeah. Now, I can barely keep up with this one."

"Right." I had no doubt my father was doing just fine there. He'd always been a wild one.

I held up the remote about to turn the television back on, but his words halted me. "Your mother came by the house the other day."

My mother. Right. That was not the word I would use for her.

"Oh really? She need money?"

Dad's tone turned somber. One thing I knew was that he loved my mother, even being the flighty bitch that she was, he loved her. He'd wanted her from the moment he saw her, and she gave in for awhile. But like everything else, she picked up and took off. A free spirit I was told over and over again. Bullshit. She just didn't want any responsibilities.

She'd come by every now and then, but never stayed too long. My kids met her a couple of times, but she was just a stranger to them. Fuck, she was a stranger to me. Never had her more than a few days here and there during my entire childhood.

"Yeah." He huffed out a breath. "Said the spirit was telling her to go to North Carolina for a while and needed help gettin' there. Since I don't want her ass here near you or my grandkids, I gave it to her, and she blew out as fast as she came in."

"Shouldn't give that woman money, Dad. She's a waste of space."

His head turned to me, brow raised. "You have every right to feel that way, but she did love you with everything inside of her."

"Yeah, when I was born. After that... she flew."

My father raised me on his own with the help of the club since I was born. Mom would come and go a few days here and there until Dad put an end to it, meeting her at other places as not to hurt me as I got older and started asking questions. Hell, I didn't care to remember any of that shit.

I had one parent, and he was in the seat next to me. The only one who mattered.

"Yeah. It's better this way."

"Dad, I'm serious. Don't give her anymore money.

She has a problem she can come to me about it. She doesn't need to be bothering you."

Honestly, I'd love it if the bitch came to me so I could tell her to piss off. My father would want to coddle her like every other time. True, he didn't want the woman around me or my kids, but he still loved her to this day. He never denied it, but I'd never asked either.

He said nothing so I prompted, "Dad?"

"Yeah. I hear you."

Blowing out a heavy sigh, I let it drop and asked, "You goin' to Greer's game tomorrow night?"

"You know I don't miss a single game. Is my girl gonna be there?"

I clicked on the television back to the game. "Doubtful. Jenny doesn't let her out much. Greer says he needs to talk to me about something, though. Hell if I know what it's about. He didn't say, but he sounded worried."

"He doesn't have some girl knocked up, does he?"

A chuckle escaped. "Great minds think alike, old man. I said the same shit to him, but he gets me and knows I'll beat his ass if he ends up being a dad in high school."

"Don't want him following the path his dad did, huh?"

"Fuck no. Love my boy, but having him while

Sophia and I were in high school kicked both of our asses."

He looked over. "Yeah, it did. But you pulled your shit together and now have a very strong independent kid on your hands."

"Yeah. He's good."

On the screen the Crimson Tide ran in for a thirty-seven-yard touchdown. Fuck yeah!

"Now your girl…"

He let that hang in the air clogging up the space around us and taking the excitement of the touchdown out of my head. Van's mother was a piece of shit junkie who had repeatedly told me she was pulling her head out of her ass, would get clean, and get rid of that jackass she'd been letting stay at the house. It hadn't happened yet.

I'd give anything for Sophia to be Van's mother. Sophia had her shit going on and her head screwed on straight.

Jenny did not and was a pain in my ass. She stayed away, for the most part.

Greer though, he wasn't going to go through the same shit I had. That kid had better not tell me he's gonna be a daddy. Wasn't that the thing about life? Each generation wanting the next to do better than the one before. If I could scare the shit out of my boy, I would do it in a heartbeat.

"What?" I prompted him.

"Need to get a tighter rein on that mother."

I turned to him away from the television. "What'd you hear?"

Dad shook his head. "Jenny."

If the man could be any more vague, it would be a miracle. There was so much goin' on with that bitch. I didn't have to wait long though, because he continued. "That dickhead is still in her house and from talk, he's not goin' anywhere."

"Fuck." The bitch promised me that she'd have my ten-year-old little girl out of that damn house and away from her fuckwad of a boyfriend. "Guess it's time I make him go and put her ass in rehab myself."

Dad nodded. "Yep. Either that or you take Van out of there."

"Don't you think she should be with her mother and do all that girl shit?" I asked, really wanting to know this answer. His opinion and thoughts were very important to me, and I sucked them in down to my bones. Van being with her mother was questionable because the parent role was reversed in that home. I fucking hated it.

"Not if she's in a house with a dick like Stan and Jenny stays."

"That's the club's fuckin' house she lives in."

He put his beer to his lips and took a pull. "Know that, son. What're you gonna do about it?"

"Piss the bitch off more."

"Exactly. Van can hang out with your old man. Know you're busy."

"Thanks. Anything else I need to know from your fucked up wisdom bank?"

He chuckled.

"Can we stop talkin' about this shit and watch the game?"

"Yeah."

That was what we did. Our heartfelt conversation over, we watched the red blow the other team out of the water.

Roll Tide, Rebellion, Alabama life.

8

Crow

"Nothin'," Phoenix called out after breaking open the safe upstairs in the hall closet. What was the point of a safe if you didn't even keep your kids' birth certificates or social security cards in them? I never understood that. Seemed stupid to me. Not that the information would help us any. Just common sense.

Lemon was on the computer seeing what he could find, while Wrong Way, Tex, Hornet, Rooster and Brewer were scoping out the house.

The prospect called twenty minutes ago stating the woman packed up her kids in the minivan and left. It took us ten to get here. The woman really needed a new security system. The one she had was shit and got popped in less than a minute.

Thumbing through the papers in the filing cabinet, the woman had a serious spending habit and kept every fucking credit card bill, all filed exactly in order. On the Visa charge, there was a spot for Berry that listed everything he bought or went using the card.

Pulling them from the confines it showed that yes, in fact, he stopped using that card about four months ago. Therefore, looking at the later ones became a priority trying to find out if there was a pattern.

Grabbing my phone, I snapped pictures of all the charges going back a year, intent on giving them to Wrong Way to decipher because nothing stood out like a sore thumb at first glance.

"Picture!" Hornet called out as I made my way into the living room where he stood, a picture off the wall and a safe behind it.

Phoenix came grabbing his tools and getting to work. Fifteen seconds later, it was popped open. Inside was cash. A lot of cash. Stacks of hundreds each bound into five thousand increments. There had to be ninety grand in there.

Other than that, there was nothing. Why would she have this much cash? The bigger question was did she know she had this much cash or was this all her husband?

It left me with more questions than answers.

"Take it. We'll see who it belongs to. If it's the wife, she'll file a report. If it's him, we'll know he's around."

Hornet nodded and pulled out the bills.

We could always use more cash.

THE STADIUM WAS PACKED to capacity, and it was standing room only. It didn't matter to me because no one was stupid enough to sit in our section. We'd donated a fuck load of money to this school and it came with some perks. Prized seats at the fifty-yard line. Not that even if we didn't give money, we wouldn't sit where the fuck we wanted.

High school seemed so damn long ago and here I was with a junior in it. Had him when I was way too fuckin' young, but he was one of the best things that happened to me. Fucking loved my kids.

Not what they did sometimes, but kids were kids and all that shit.

Entering the stands, Sophia, Greer's mom, sat in our section on the very first row of bleachers where she sat at every single game. She smiled as we walked up to her.

"Hey," I said, wrapping my hand around her head, pulling it to me and kissing the top of her hair as she then smiled up at me.

"Hey, yourself."

That smile of hers was what pulled me to her back in high school. Hell, pulled everyone. One look and I was hooked. Add in her chestnut hair, blue eyes, and curvaceous body, she was a knockout. Still was even after all these years. Sophia took care of herself in every way, still as beautiful as ever.

Our relationship didn't survive after we graduated. We held our shit together for Greer, but Sophia needed a different man than who I was. She wanted the man who was going to settle down at eighteen, get a steady job, and be there for dinner every night at five pm.

She knew that mold didn't fit me, but thought she could change me, making me into who she wanted and needed.

Even at eighteen, I knew what I wanted and where my life was going to take me. I'd told her repeatedly, but it wasn't what she envisioned in her life. She didn't want to be part of a motorcycle club or anything that went along with it.

We'd argue all the damn time about it, her thinking one day I'd change my mind and me knowing it wasn't going to happen. My kid was important to me and I'd been a staple in his life every day. Sophia and I together though, was a recipe for disaster.

She was a damn good woman then and now. Between us we worked hard to make our lives flow together these past sixteen years. Our relationship changed to friends instead of lovers. It didn't happen overnight and we both had a temper so times on occasion, were bad.

Now though, we worked as a team. She respected my life, and I respected hers.

Sophia had been married once, but now divorced. She had a daughter named Lucia, who was around ten and spent the weekends with her father. He was a dick. I had zero use for him and was happy when she got shot of him three years ago.

I took my seat behind her as my brothers gathered around taking their spots on the hard bleachers. My father pulled up the rear, leaned down and kissed Sophia on the cheek before moving up to sit.

He had a very soft spot for Sophia. Hell, I did too. Good women tend to get those from men like us.

Setting a hand on her shoulder, I leaned down to her ear. "Greer's comin' to my place after. You good with that?"

She turned, her face very close to mine, those plump lips I remembered all too well red and wet. "Yeah. He told me. I'm having a quiet night in after this. Lucia is with her father."

Sophia was a damn good mom to both of her kids. Loved them with everything she had inside of her and would give them the world. She was very active in their school and knew everything going on.

"Nice. You hangin' in there? Need anything?" I asked, knowing that she had money. One, because I sent it to her every month and two, she had a great job at the local insurance company. Not to mention, her dick of an ex-husband had to pay her child support and alimony; my attorney at the time made sure of it.

Sophia and I were long over, but I'd always take care of her.

Her head shook. "We're good." Sweet. Too damn sweet to be mixed up with the likes of me, but part of my family all the same. I hoped one day she would find herself a good man who did right by her.

"You call me, you need anything." She nodded as the game started, focusing all the attention around us to the boys on the field.

Ravage had a shit ton going on, but I told my boy I'd be here, so I was.

Fourth quarter, the Panthers were up by three and needed to make a touchdown to seal the deal. The play set into motion, the ball flying in the sky directly into my boy's arms in the end zone. The crowd around us went wired, slamming their feet on the metal bleachers and screaming at the top of their lungs. The colors red and white twirled in the air from the cloths the cheerleaders sold and made a mint.

Greer had a wide smile on his face as his team-mates slapped his helmet in congratulations. The entire Panthers' side was on a high of excitement. Here in Alabama we took all football as serious as they come. None of that pussy shit. Hardcore down and out, football was as sacred as church. *Our* church that was. Panthers and Roll Tide all day every day.

Two men caught my attention walking in front of the gate on our side of the field, and everyone else around us because they were yelling very stupidly that the Panthers sucked ass. The once rowdy crowd now turned into a silent one. The men's steps were sloppy telling me they had one too many. And people said I was a dick for what I did. At least I'd never show up to my kid's game drunk off my ass making a damn scene like these fuckers.

"Get your ass on the other side of the field!" Brewer called out as the drunk guys looked up to our area, wide smiles on their faces like there was some sort of inside joke we weren't privy to. I could feel it before they did it, that gut feeling that they were going to cause trouble and were going to be in for a rude awakening. My gut was rarely wrong.

"Oh, the Panthers got themselves a gang," the tallest of the men said again stupidly, practically tripping over his feet.

I let out a low whistle. My brothers and I all rose while the two assholes were laughing and throwing their heads back, not paying a lick of attention to what was going on around them. Mistake. We got to them and stood right in their path so they had to stop and look up... all the way up to see us. They were short little fuckers. Stupid and small, never a good combination. If they weren't fast, they were really in trouble.

"What the—?" the shorter one said, halting his step and grabbing on to tall guy and finally catching his attention.

A low murmur came over the crowd, and we had no doubt every eye in that stadium including the players and coaches were on us. We were Ravage therefore not stupid enough to beat the fuck out of these two with all these witnesses. Security was supposed to be everywhere; obviously, someone was falling down on their job and would get a call Monday morning.

It made this situation our business to handle and get out of the damn stadium.

"We're your escorts," I ordered, cracking my knuckles in warning, wondering if they caught my meaning because their eyes didn't show it. Morons. Great.

"You can't make us leave!" the short one, aka stubby, yelled.

"The fuck we can't," Phoenix added into the mix. "You either walk yourselves out of here." Phoenix got very close to the men and whispered, "Or we make you." The sound was so menacing it made me smile. He was a twisted fuck, but damn happy he was on my team. He'd lived in Rebellion all his life just like me, going through this school and running this town. We didn't become close until senior year.

"You can't hurt us," the taller one, aka stick, said. "We have the right to be here. Our kids are playing."

Phoenix turned to me. "Seriously. These fuckers couldn't put two and two together."

A hand came to my shoulder, and I looked over to

Brewer. "You know we could make a citizen's arrest." To this I smiled then nodded.

The bastards yelled and screamed the entire way out of the field as we physically removed them from the game. It made me miss the last few minutes, but the Panthers won and I got to see my boy score. All was good.

When we handed them over to security with a smile, Brewer spewed some shit about a citizen's arrest. The guards did nothing but take the assholes. Sometimes being within the law worked in our favor, but this was very rare. Not gonna get arrested for something as stupid as these fucks, but if I ever saw those fuckwads again though, they'd be seeing my fists.

***

THE DOOR OPENED and Greer came through lugging his huge bag filled with football gear and no doubt smelling like shit, tossing it to the floor in the living room. My place was only a few blocks from the clubhouse. A two story, blue-gray sided home with not one bit of landscaping around it.

When I bought it, the developers had it all decked out with bushes and shrubbery. One of the prospects pulled it all out. There wasn't time to deal with shit that wasn't important. The grass got mowed and the rest of it could go to hell. I couldn't give two shits that the old lady two doors down on the opposite side of the road hated it.

It wasn't her haggard ass out there weeding and mulching all that shit.

"Hey, son. Great game." I reached out tagging my boy around his neck and bringing him close to me, giving him a squeeze. Then seeing his smile, I released him.

"Yeah. Need a shower."

He wasn't wrong. He smelled like a locker room filled with thousands of sweaty boys going through puberty and not one was wearing deodorant.

"Go. Come back and we'll talk."

He nodded and climbed his way up the stairs. Moments later the shower turned on. I grabbed a beer moving to the living room. The sectional was huge. No other way to describe it. Each of my kids and myself could lay on the fucker spread out and not touch.

Bought it just for that reason.

This room was simple. Couch, coffee table, and huge ass television with a gaming system below it. There was surround sound throughout the room allowing us to hear every crunch during a game.

Van, short for Savannah, said it needed pillows and blankets. Therefore, I gave her the cash and made Greer take her to the store. Didn't know what store and didn't give a fuck.

They came back with a shit ton of stuff, but most of

it was for their rooms here. The living room only got the necessities, pillows and blankets. They were stored in the closet mostly when my kids weren't here.

My mind spun as I took a pull on my beer. There was so much going on at one time. Waiting for information to start flowing was difficult. Thinker. That was what my father always called me growing up.

He said I used to have to think up plans for everything. Every scenario had a different outcome, and I needed to be prepared. Some things never changed. Except now things could mean life or death. Back then it was more like how to build a boat out of Legos while missing a prominent piece.

Greer came jogging down the stairs, went into the kitchen where I heard the door of the fridge open and shut, then came into the living room sitting down with a whip of wind. He tore off the top of a Gatorade and downed half of it in one gulp.

Sixteen-years-old and driving. I wasn't sure how my boy got so grown up so fast. Time ticked every second and most of the time we didn't notice.

When Greer was born, Soph and I had no clue what to do. We were so lost. Changing a diaper was an experience. Even with all our struggles as new parents, he turned out pretty fucking great.

"Son."

His eyes lifted to mine with worry etched inside of them. Open and honest was what my kids and I had.

No matter the consequences we communicated and it became a staple. It only took him a second to start. "Mom is dating someone, and I don't think he's good news."

"Okay. Why not?" Sophia sat by herself tonight. Surely whoever this asshole was wouldn't leave her to that. She was too good of a woman to be treated with utter disrespect.

"The other day when I came home from practice, Mom was gone and he was there. I found him in the office looking through some of Mom's stuff. When I went to the door and he saw me, he said he lost a fax that Mom let him put through on the machine. But, Dad, he wasn't anywhere near the fax machine."

"Did you talk to your mom?"

He shook his head. "She really likes this one, and I don't have any proof of anything. He just rubs me the wrong way. There's something off with him."

"What's his name?"

"Simon Bellville."

"That's where I'll start. If there's anything going on, I'll take care of it."

He breathed out a puff of air and leaned back in the seat. "Mom's been lonely and says she met this guy through her work, but, Dad, he doesn't work there. I don't know if he's a client or something. It's all just really off."

"How do you know he doesn't work there?"

"Google."

I smiled at my boy. The brains on him would serve him well in life. "We'll get this shit handled. No one is gonna take advantage of your mom. I promise you that."

"Thanks."

"You always come to me with this shit, Greer. I don't give a fuck what it is. You come to me."

He nodded and took another deep drink of his Gatorade.

"Right. Hungry?"

"Hell yeah," he replied.

"I'll order two pizzas." We laughed as I picked up the phone and dialed.

Time with Greer was always great. My boy was the spitting image of his dad, and I was proud of that.

In a few days, it was go time for the run for Xavier and Marcus. Everything had better go fucking smooth or blood would be shed and not Ravage blood.

I always came home to my kids. I lived for my club, bled for them, but my heart beat for my children. Always.

9

Rylynn

KNOCKING ON THE DOOR HARDER, STILL NO ONE SHOWED up at Penny's house. She was the last one who admitted to being with Elizabeth that night she disappeared. If they were the best of friends, my thought would be that Penny knew more than she stated in the report.

Which wasn't much to begin with. Penny picked Elizabeth up around seven thirty that night from Elizabeth's house. They went to The Junction, a local teen hotspot, and grabbed a bite to eat. After that they went to the party at Jonny Walp's home. They drank beer, played games, and talked to, according to her, everyone at the party. She said that Elizabeth was very well liked by everyone and stopped all the time to talk to people.

Penny stated that Elizabeth went into the bathroom. She saw her go in and waited outside the door.

Two boys came up and tried talking to her, but she said she just smiled at them. After a while, she knocked on the door, but Elizabeth didn't answer.

Concerned, she went and found Jonny who got the door unlocked. When they looked in the room, the window was open and Elizabeth was gone.

Penny stated that she looked everywhere for her inside the house and outside. She even took drives around the area to see if she could find her.

Moving around the side of the house and looking in the windows, I didn't see anyone home. There was furniture and the last name Rager was on the mailbox. I assumed the family still lived here. I'd need to try back.

Walking back to my Jeep, I pulled the file out that was full of papers. I'd printed them all off because I needed to organize it in a way that I could understand. Everything Naddy sent me was just lumped together leading me on a wild goose chase with sections of reports in every which way. It was a mess.

Now it was in a way I could understand it.

The picture of Elizabeth Jenkins tumbled out, and I sucked in a breath. Her blonde hair was the shade of Mazie's and it made me suck in a breath every time. The picture looked of innocence with a pure complexion and very symmetrical face.

It was a school photo taken this past year before she

went missing. Her smile looked happy and true, not fake or trying too hard to be something she wasn't. Her friends described her as an honest girl who never met a person she didn't get along with. She was bubbly and energetic, but from several sources she didn't drink alcohol, but Penny said they did. A discrepancy in the story there.

The cops had witness statements and interviewed all of the kids that were at this party, including Jonny's parents who didn't know he was having a party. Lots of kids saw her at this party saying they just had small talk with her, nothing too serious.

As I read through the police records with each of the witnesses, my mind rolled through the possibilities of what could've happened that night. Having been to a shit ton of parties, there were some frightening thoughts.

The detectives on the case said that all leads were exhausted, but there had to be something that was overlooked or we'd know what happened to this girl.

And my bet was Penny. Best friends always told each other everything. There were so many more questions that needed to be asked that I was surprised the detectives on the case didn't ask. But that wasn't happening today.

Jeep in drive and the folder on the passenger seat, I set off for home. My cell rang, the display saying *Nox Calling.*

"Hey there, handsome," I teased, answering the line.

"Ry." He paused.

"Yeah, Nox. What's up?"

My gut twisted, and the hairs on the back of my neck rose. The seriousness of his tone had me on edge. What if something happened to my dad? Mom? Mazie? Grandma? Anyone at the club? No. This couldn't be happening again. It was too raw still.

Breathing in and out deeply, I pulled my head out of my ass. This wasn't me, dammit.

"It's done," he said cryptically.

"What?"

"He's been avenged."

Quickly, I pulled off the side of the road, my hands shaking. Being cut out of the loop when it came to killing my grandpa was difficult. I had to look really deep within myself to find the courage to step back. It was so fucking hard. Every instinct inside of me screamed for action. For vengeance.

It was the moment that I really understood the club business aspect of the Ravage MC. It was deeper than I'd been taught throughout the years. While my mom would always say that Dad was on club business, that business didn't affect me. Therefore, I let it go my mind conjuring up all kinds of things.

Not being naïve to it, but also not fully one hundred percent getting it either.

Until this. Until some dickhead killed my grandpa and injured my grandma.

Club business meant retribution for those members of the family hurt or murdered. It was an impact all itself.

"Really?"

"Just between you and me, Ry. Got me?" he said. There was no way in hell I'd say anything to anyone. Nox was doing something he shouldn't do, I knew it, and I was so damn grateful he told me.

"Never a word."

Tears streamed down my cheeks as sadness and relief warred with each other. Two opposite feelings, yet the same as well. My grandpa could rest in peace now knowing whoever took him from us was gone and could never hurt anyone again.

"Later."

"Later." My *later* was a bit choky.

Disconnecting, I tossed the phone into the cup holder, laid my head back on the headrest, and closed my eyes.

Closure. It would never seal the wound completely, but it was a start.

It was exactly what I needed to give Elizabeth Jenkins' family. And I would.

10

Crow

"I'm done with your shit."

The glare Jenny gave me did nothing but piss me off more. She was high as a kite, on what who the fuck knew. She smoked or snorted anything she could get her hands on. Some asshole could crush up Tic Tacs and tell her it would give her the best high of her life, and she'd find the money to buy it.

Unfortunately, it was usually money that I'd given her for Van which only meant I was enabling her. But fuck, what the hell was a dad supposed to do?

I knew the answer to that, and it needed to happen.

"Crow, I can't go to rehab." Jenny started crying as the side door opened and her loser of a boyfriend Stan walked in. Great, two junkies to deal with. Jenny went to Stan. "Tell him. Tell him I can't go to rehab. I have to work."

"Work? Where the fuck do you work?" I clipped out, knowing damn well she didn't have a fucking job. She got fired from the last one for showing up to work high. Go figure.

Jenny's eyes flicked back and forth between Stan and myself, indecision in them.

"Leave her the fuck alone and go," Stan said.

In a flash, his shirt was gripped in my fist and my face in his. I slammed his head against the wall. "You forget who owns this house, motherfucker. It sure as shit ain't you." I slammed him again. "You get your shit and be moved out tonight. You are not to step foot in this place or I swear to Christ, you'll be dead."

I slammed him once more, releasing him to stumble away from me.

"Why did you do that!" Jenny shrieked. The bitch gave me a headache every time I was near her.

"Shut the fuck up." I glared at her and finally she listened. "You're gonna pack your clothes, get in the van outside, and it's gonna take you to rehab. You'll stay there until you can lay off the shit."

"I can't," she said immediately. "I... I..."

The thing that really stood out to me was her first words weren't that she had to take care of Van, who was luckily at school. No, it was all about her. Selfish and self-centered. Not a good role model for Van.

While I'd be gone a lot, she could be with my old

man. We'd make this shit work. Anything was better than her living in this hell hole.

"Bitch," I growled.

"I can't go. We'll lose the house!"

This made me still. There was no way this could even be a possibility. The house wasn't under her name in any way, shape, or form.

"What did you say?" I bit off, needing her to fill in the blanks here.

She went white as a sheet, no doubt pissed that she said anything at all. Too late. "I…"

"Tell me!" I roared this time.

She jumped back then said, "We have a loan on the house, and I can't go away because we need the money you give me to pay it back."

I took a menacing step forward. "You did what exactly?"

Stan appeared in the doorway. "Jenny, shut up," he barked. In two steps, he was on the floor, my fist connecting with his temple.

"Tell me, now!"

A tear slid down Jenny's cheek, but it wasn't sadness—it was fear. True unadulterated fear. She took a step back. "We went to Ebony. She gave us a loan."

Fuck. "How is that possible? She only gives out loans if you have collateral. I own your car, and the club owns this house. There's nothing you have of value to put up."

Her eyes darted around the room focusing on Stan, but he was out cold. "Nothin' is gettin' you out of this, Jenny," I warned.

"The house. Stan put together some papers that said we were the owners. She took them and gave us the money." Respect was a huge thing in my world, right up there with loyalty. I'd always had respect for women as long as they respected me. Never put a hand on a woman in anger, ever.

It was taking every bit of control in my body not to wrap my hands around this bitch's throat and squeeze the life out of her. Always knew the bitch was dumb, but this layer of dumb was a new low.

"You mean to tell me you forged paperwork claiming you two idiots were the owners of this house and used it to get money to shoot up your fuckin' arm!" The rage flowed through my veins, and I had to ball up my fists in order to keep them under control.

"We had to!"

"Bitch, you fuckin' did not. This is jacked even for your ass." I took a step back and took a deep breath. "You have no option. You're goin' to rehab right now. You stay until you're clean, or this house and all the shit in it is gone. Van is gone. No more chances. No more anything."

Jenny was full out crying now as she moved to Stan and sunk to the floor next to him.

"Bitch, I can't believe you went to Ebony." Ebony

was a loan shark who was high up on the food chain because she'd made a mint off assholes like these, not being able to pay her back and confiscating their shit then selling it. She was straight no holds barred. Now, I was going to need to meet up with her and fix this problem.

Like I needed another damn thing on my fucking plate. Fuck.

"I'm sorry," she cried, but I was done.

"Let's go. Now."

"You can't..." Stan started getting back to his feet, but I pulled out my gun. This dog and pony show was over with.

"Fucker, you tell me I can't do somethin' one more time, I'll start takin' off your body parts one by fuckin' one."

He halted and took a step back.

In the other hand, I grabbed my cell calling Hornet and Rooster. "Come get her."

Two seconds later the guys came in, lifting a sobbing Jenny. "Take her to Convorse."

"You want her that far away?" Hornet asked.

"If I could get the bitch further away in this short of time, I'd fuckin' do it."

"Right," he answered and took Jenny out. Fuck her clothes. She could live naked for all I cared.

Staring Stan in the eye, two shots went right to his head as he fell to the ground in a heap. Fucker messed with Ravage putting out house up so he could shoot it or snort it. Fuck him.

Punching in Phoenix's number, he answered on the second ring.

"Need you at Jenny's house. Stan needs help gettin' out of the house. Bring a tarp."

"That sounds like a shit job." He chuckled.

"One that you like doin'."

"Be there in ten."

I disconnected the phone turning to the heap on the floor. That was going to be a bitch to get out of the carpet.

Five minutes later Phoenix was there. Five minutes after that, I was packing my daughter's stuff and shoving it in my Tahoe. It wasn't everything, but it was the important shit. Fifteen minutes after that, I was picking my girl up at school to bring her home.

"AND WHO IS THIS?" I asked, entering my house with my son sitting at the table with a beautiful young woman with brunette hair. At least they were at the table and not back in his room.

"Greer!" Van screamed at the top of her lungs, running into her brother's arms and wrapping him up tight. She adored her big brother, and it had been awhile since they were together here. This would be good for the both of them.

"Hey, peanut. Didn't know you'd be here." His eyes jetting back and forth between his sister and me. He knew Jenny, and I'd tell him later. I shook my head.

"Yeah! I get to stay with Daddy and then Grandpa!"

"That's awesome."

She released her brother and looked to the girl next him. "Hi." She did the little wave thing that little girls do. It was cute. I wanted her to stay little for as long as possible. At Jenny's she didn't have that. The roles were reversed and Van was the caretaker. It had to end.

"Dad, peanut, this is Aubrey, the tutor I told you about, Dad."

She smiled softly and as I made it to the table, I spoke, "Welcome. We're counting on you for Greer here to pass math. You sure you're up for that challenge?"

Her smile widened. "I'm gonna give it a shot."

"That's a pretty name. I'm Van." Van introduced herself with a smile.

"Nice to meet you." Aubrey smiled then turned back to the paper as Greer winked at me.

"Out here only," I ordered Greer who shook his head, but did it laughing. He wouldn't be laughing when he ended up being a dad at sixteen.

"Go wash up, Van. I'll bring your stuff in."

"Okay!" She took off happily thinking this was a little vacation getting to spend time with the men in her life. Soon, I'd tell her she wasn't going back there, but now wasn't the time.

Lugging in the boxes, my mind rolled around everything going on with the club and at home.

We were still waiting for someone to report the money missing at the Alabaster home and were keeping our eyes and ears open for whoever was supposedly looking for us. Tommy was in luck because we had a run tomorrow, so he had a few extra days to pull his head out of his ass and get us what we needed.

My two kids under the same roof. It felt good, but there was something still missing. One day at a time. That was all we could do.

11

Rylynn

CLIENT NUMBER ONE CALLED ME EARLIER SAYING HER husband was going on a business trip and gave me the ins and outs of his schedule. I was on the road tailing this guy who didn't go over sixty-five miles an hour driving me nuts. Did he not know what a gas pedal was?

Since waking up this morning in a hotel on the boarder of Georgia and Alabama, this guy had done nothing wrong that I could see. He was B-O-R-I-N-G. He was in his hotel alone, my room had a good view of his window. I peeped and went into the offices only to come out hours later, went to get food, and then back to the office.

Currently, he was eating a Ruben sandwich in a greasy spoon, and I was four booths behind him watching. With a college sweatshirt and my hair up in a messy bun up on top, I looked invisible, blending into the surroundings. Now if I would've come in with all black on, that would have made me stick out like a sore thumb.

It was something I'd learned along the way, mostly by watching my father. How to be stealthy. How to blend into the crowd and become a nobody that no one would remember. Be seen, but not. It wasn't an easy task and I'd failed several times, but with each attempt, I got better.

This guy was driving me to think about changing careers. I almost wished he had something exciting happen during this trip so I could do something. His wife said he goes back tomorrow morning and he'd done nothing but work, eat, and sleep. No woman on the side for him.

Taking a bite of my burger with ketchup, I looked around the place not even knowing what it was called. Judging from the beat-up booths and torn vinyl on the chairs, it'd been around for quite a long time.

Seeing the glob of dust above the window the waitresses and cooks used to put the food out, I went back to my burger trying to forget it. Lord knew what I put into my mouth, but it tasted damn good. Funny how a greasy spoon burger always hit the spot, drunk or not.

My guy hadn't moved other than to pick up his damn sandwich. He kept looking down, playing on his phone. Maybe texting his chick on the side? Who was I kidding. This guy didn't have anything anywhere.

A bell rang over the door, my eyes instantly darting to it. The burger froze midway to my mouth, breaths seized and muscles went tight.

The Ravage Rebellion came through, Crow the third one in. He was smiling at something the guy behind him said. That smile was killer, and I hadn't forgotten it a single moment since he left me on my doorstep.

My heartbeat picked up, and I felt the blush heat my cheeks just in watching him from afar.

He was so gorgeous—strong arms, hair tousled from the wind of riding, leather fitting him like a glove along with jeans that had tears in them every which way. My body throbbed craving him, wanting him.

It wasn't until he turned my way and our eyes connected seeing the stunned look on his face that I became unstuck. Shit, shit, shit!

His strides were long, and I knew he was going to blow my cover. There was nowhere to hide and nowhere to go. Blowing my cover wasn't an option. This husband was already boring enough, and I wanted to be done with it. If Crow exposed me, I wouldn't be able to get this close to the guy again and get this job finished. Shit.

I launched myself out of the booth and flew into Crow's arms, jumping up and wrapping my legs around his hips. He caught me with ease, and I could feel his laughter against my breasts causing my nipples to harden.

"Act like you're here for me. Have one of your guys grab my bag and carry me out of here," I whispered in his ear, trying desperately not to smell him but coming up short. Dirt, air, sun, leather and Crow was what he smelled like, stirring my body up.

"What's the deal, Pixie?" His hands squeezed my ass, and my hips of their own volition began to move feeling his hardness. Snapping myself out of it, I hoisted myself up more so I couldn't feel his cock and burrowed my face in his neck to not be seen.

"Please, Crow. I'll explain everything once you get me out of here," I pleaded into his neck, my lips touching there bringing his taste inside me once again.

"You in trouble?" he asked, and I wanted to roll my eyes. Why was that always the first thing that men thought? Couldn't a woman not be a damsel in distress? Just out doing her job? Not every woman needed a man to rescue them.

"No. Just please do this for me. Swear I'll explain."

"Only if I'm in your bed tonight," he responded, and my body stilled. It took everything inside of me not to look up into his eyes. What I wanted to see there, I wasn't sure, but good or bad part of me was dying to know.

"What?" I asked, stunned as my body flared, excitedly anticipating what Crow would do in my bed. Who was I kidding? I knew exactly what he'd do to me. Fuck me until I couldn't move. Which wouldn't be such a bad thing.

"You heard me, Pixie. Tell me your answer."

Shit, shit, shit. It wasn't like this was our first time together. It was really a no-brainer.

"Fine. Just get me out of here." His smell was overpowering me, and I needed fresh air to clear my head. Crow could not scramble my brain cells.

"Fuck you feel good, baby." He did too. My vixen hips wanted so badly to grind on him.

"What's going on here?" I heard a deep voice ask with humor lighting his tone.

I felt Crow's laugh once again. "Phoenix, grab that bag." His head moved, but I kept my face inside his neck shielding me from everything.

"This isn't funny," I said against his neck.

"This is fuckin' hilarious," he responded.

We were on the move, heading out the door and into the parking lot. "You have a specific place you want me to take ya? I mean this is fun and all, but I'd rather have my cock inside of you."

"Would you stop?"

"No." He was blunt as usual. I growled and he laughed, "Now who's Grizzly?"

"Did you see that guy in there with the wine-colored shirt, sitting alone four booths in front of me?"

I felt his neck twist. "Yeah. Doesn't look like your type, babe."

"Yeah, I go more for the Smurf type. All small and blue balled."

He laughed hard shaking my body.

"Would you pay attention?" I clipped.

"I am, Pixie. You're just damn funny."

He was pushing every fucking button inside of me, and I loved it and hated it at the same time. "Take me somewhere that he won't see my face."

He sobered turning all business, his voice and body coming alert, but kept moving. "He givin' you shit?"

"No. He's my target." My back was pressed against something hard and only then did I lift my head from his neck, trusting that Crow did as I'd asked. Crow's face was fierce and so damn hot. My lips tingled wanting to kiss him.

I sucked in a deep breath of fresh air, but it did nothing to quench the thirst I had for this man.

"Talk to me," he ordered, his hands gripping my ass tighter in a warning that also shown on his face. He was ready to rip this guy apart, and there was no need for that.

"Can you put me down?" I asked, but he didn't move. I felt the stares from several of his brothers. Looking up, I wasn't wrong. Crow's hand came to my face, and he turned it so my eyes were focused on him.

"No, and start fuckin' talkin'."

Letting out a heavy sigh, I talked, but it wasn't what he wanted to hear. "He's my husband and I was waiting for his tramp to show up so I could beat her ass."

Crow didn't think what I said was funny one bit. Guess the sarcasm train had left the depot. His brothers said nothing. Right now, dealing with a man who was all man and wouldn't take any shit—even from someone like me—probably wasn't my best reply.

I shook my head all the while watching his expressions wanting to gauge his level of angry from miffed to infuriated. If I had to try to hold him back, I knew it wouldn't go well, but the guy I was tailing hadn't hurt me. "Got it. He's my target. I'm a private investigator. His wife hired me to follow him on a business trip to catch him in the act of fuckin' around on her."

The stony look smoothed out just a bit, but the edge was still there. "You're chasin' someone in a town you aren't familiar with, alone? What the fuck, Rylynn?"

Now, he was beyond pissed, and his grip on me tightened to almost the point of pain, but I ignored it. "I'm a big girl, Crow, and I'm doin' my job. This is how I make a living."

"You chase assholes down and what, take pictures of them?"

"Can you put me down?"

His tone was a bit condescending, and I didn't care for that much.

My back was pressed harder into the concrete, his chest pressing into mine. Fuck, how could I be pissed and be hot for at him at the same time?

"I fuckin' said no. I should turn your ass over my knee."

"Love to see you try it, big man, but that ain't happenin'. Put me down," I barked louder and felt the air around us tense. I knew why. This was the president of the Ravage Rebellions MC. No one talked to him like that, and here I was some woman that really none of his brothers knew who was standing up to their leader. I'd grown up my entire life being around men who were real men and knew the boundaries. But I was getting angry. I mean, who did this guy think he was? He sure as shit wasn't my keeper. "Now."

"I don't know if I should throttle you, fuck you, or kill you."

This made me laugh for some insane reason, pissing Crow off more. "Pixie," he growled.

My laughs calmed, and I sucked in a deep breath. "Look. Yes. I'm here tailin' this guy to get pictures of him cheating, but since he's boring as fuck, I've been just babysitting. He goes back tomorrow morning, and so do I. It's all good."

"It is not all good." He released my ass, my legs falling to the ground and catching me, but he didn't let me go. Instead, he whipped me around and pulled my back to his front to face his brothers.

I only knew one of them, Brewer because he was the vice president. The others I had no clue, but I didn't cower. No man wanted a woman who would couldn't stand on her own two feet. Lucky for me I'd had a lot of practice between my father and Cruz; it was a given.

The all stared at me trying to place me, and I lifted my chin. Crow introduced them. "This is Brewer, Wrong Way, Rooster, Hornet, Tex and Lemon. I nodded as he pointed to each one.

Brewer's head tipped to the side, light dawning. "Fuck. You're Rhys' kid."

A smile crept up my lips. Maybe some women would get pissed or frustrated to be connected to their parents. But not me. I was happy to be my father's kid. Happy to be in the Ravage MC. There was nothing there that made me feel in anyway like his words were an insult.

"Christ, Crow. Did you fuck her?" a man with dark black hair said as he looked at our stance. The look on his face was interesting, but I couldn't tell which way he was going with it. He was introduced as Phoenix. "Fuck, even I'm not that crazy."

I decided to speak. "Actually, my inner hellcat was let loose, and I climbed him like a tree."

Chuckles spread through the guys, and I was happy they got my meaning. Like I said, sometimes people got it and other times they didn't.

Crow's grip tightened putting pressure at my chest, gaining me his attention. "Had you purrin' just fine," he said slowly in my ear nipping my lobe. My knees tried to give out, but I held strong.

"Never said you didn't." Then I turned my head around to him and peered into his eyes. "Why are you here? Rebellion is three and a half hours away." I winked. "Or three if I'm driving."

His eyes flared in that sexy way, like when he came deep inside me. "Club business."

I broke his spell by turning back to the guys. Those were the magic words for me to shut up and mind my own business. "Right. Okay, I need to get to my Jeep so I'm ready to roll when this guy leaves."

Crow's arm tensed, but didn't release me. "You think for one fuckin' second I'm lettin' you go so you can follow this asshole to his piece or wherever? I'll tie you to the back of my bike before that happens, Pixie."

I smirked, kind of liking that idea, and turned in his arms. "While I'm happy to be tied up, I need to get the goods on this guy, or by the way this is going, not getting the goods on him so I can close this case and get paid."

"That's. Not. Gonna. Happen," Crow growled. He had to bend down slightly to get in my face, and I was a tall woman. It made the movement all that more intriguing. His words should piss me off as he was again telling me what I was going to do; instead, they made me wet. Full out if I could get some friction between my legs, I'd come, wet.

Shit, all this guy had to do was breathe on me and I was turned on. Touch me and I wanted to purr like a damn kitten.

Off to the side a car started up, and I swung my head to the noise seeing it was my guy. I tried to break out of Crow's arms, but he refused.

"Crow. Let me go. That's my guy!"

I felt my body jolt as Crow fell back into the wall. His arms came up capturing mine, and one of his legs swung around pinning me to him. He had me completely and totally under his control.

Glaring at him, my nostrils flared as I turned just in time to see my guy drive out of the lot.

My eyes went back to Crow's to see him grinning. "Told ya, you're done with this."

"Are you telling me, a man whom I've slept with once, that I'm done with a job?"

"Yep."

My glare turned into a snarl. "Do I come to your clubhouse and tell you that you can't do your job?"

"Nope."

"Then what makes you think you can do it to me?"

I struggled a little to try to get free, but he had me captured so I stopped since it wasn't worth my energy when a bigger argument was meant to be had.

Crow looked over my shoulder and spoke, "Call the prospects. Get them on the road to get Ry's Jeep."

"What?" I hissed. "There's no reason for them to drive three hours to get a car when I'm standing right here and can drive perfectly fine."

"On it," heard one of the guys say as I glared at the man in front of me.

"Told you, you're on the back of my bike."

I felt my body tense because he didn't say that. He said he would tie me to him on his bike. Being around bikers my whole life, I'd heard lots of different terms. Some of my father's associates used and others they did not. This was one that wasn't said much around me at home, but I knew what it meant.

I knew that the words were powerful and held so much meaning my chest clenched at the though. 'Being on the back of a man's bike' meant he wanted me. As in me with him. He couldn't be serious. It didn't make any sense whatsoever. We'd had one night together. One hot, amazing night, but there was no way he meant what I'd thought.

"Crow?"

"We're goin' back to your hotel. Now."

"But, Crow..."

"No, Rylynn. Not fuckin' playin' with you." His tone was dead serious, and I knew from experience this was something I couldn't cute or sass my way out of. Shit.

His head lifted as he looked behind me. "Recon. Get back to the hotel. Meet in the morning."

"Oh shit," I heard from someone. Then a "Got it boss." And a "On it."

It was Brewer who came up and stood beside us, his focus on Crow, not me. "This what you want?"

Crow's eyes turned sharply to his brother and I tensed, the effect hitting me in the gut. Yeah, Crow wasn't playing here. Not one little bit.

"Got it," Brewer said. "Call if ya need anything."

"Later," Crow growled then turned back to me. His lips came down hard on mine, stealing my breath just like all the kisses he'd given me before. My body began to relax at the feel, but just as soon as he started, he pulled away.

"Back of my bike, Ry. Now."

At the intensity and overall aura around him, I just nodded as he let me go, but grabbed my hand and dragged me around the building. I tugged a bit, his head whipping around. "Crow, I need my bag."

Motorcycles just started up, and Crow whistled loudly gaining their attention. "Bag!" he called out, and one of the brothers tossed it in our direction. I made a move to grab it, but Crow's hand was out and beat me to it. He reached in and grabbed my keys, tossing them back to the guy.

Shit. The man was as serious as a heart attack. But I wasn't scared; no, I was intrigued. This man, huge and imposing, was a mystery, and I always loved a good puzzle. This was bad. Very, very bad.

"Thank you," I whispered as he handed it to me, only letting me go to get on his bike. I didn't dilly and swung my leg over the ride, wrapping my arms around his stomach.

"Where?" he asked before firing the bike up.

"Holiday Inn on West Court."

He nodded as if he knew this area well, fired up the bike, and we took off like a shot. This was different than our first ride together. That time we were both horny as hell and wanted to be fucking as soon as physically possible.

I rubbed my pussy back and forth over his seat trying to get the friction I needed to come. It was out of reach though that night.

This time, I was able to enjoy the ride with Crow.

My body was thrumming for him, but it was knowing the pleasure we could give each other that made me relax and take everything in.

What in the fuck was going on here? Oh yeah, I was in serious trouble.

12

Crow

She was going over my knee first thing when we stepped into that room. Working a job in a town she didn't know on her own, and unless she had a fucking gun in her bag, she was out of her damn mind. Hell, even with it she was.

Rylynn should know better than most what could happen to a woman out on her own without anyone at her back. She'd lived this life. It wasn't a shock or a surprise. She didn't get all jumpy with anything about the club. When I told her club business, she shut it down quickly. She knew and fuck if that didn't feel good.

With her being this fucking smart, why in the fuck was she doing this shit? While she looked like she could handle herself, with her toned arms and legs, I didn't like it. I didn't like her being alone. I didn't like her in any ounce of danger. I just didn't fucking like it. It only took one second, one act, and she'd be dead. The thought of that made me sick to my stomach.

The bike swung into the parking lot, and I felt Rylynn's head twist this way, no doubt looking for the car that asshole was in. Sure enough, I saw it off to the right parked. Rylynn must've seen it too because she sank into me.

Parking, she got off and I followed behind.

"Crow," she started, but I interrupted, "Room key and number," holding out my hand. She dug in her back jeans pocket and pulled out a white card handing it to me.

"Four seventeen." She didn't hesitate and I pushed us through the lobby to the elevator, up and into her room. Not until the door latched behind me did I turn to Rylynn who looked like a deer in headlights. It made me wonder what I looked like.

Tearing off my leather I prowled to her. She was my prey, and I needed inside of her. Now.

"Crow. What..."

"Clothes off. Now."

Her eyes widened and beautiful lips parted. Fuck, she was sexy, my cock already trying to escape and meet its target. I didn't make it wait long as off came my boots, socks, jeans, underwear and shirt in seconds.

"Holy shit," Rylynn whispered, eyes wide, nipples

hard through her shirt showing me just how aroused she was.

"You're still dressed," I said expectantly, but her expression was filled with awe. "Not like you haven't seen me before, babe." I stalked to her watching as she swallowed hard liking what she saw.

"Right, but you never tore your clothes off like they were burning your skin before."

Reaching her I whipped off her shirt and tugged at her bra, getting it to release her breasts giving a soft bounce. "That's because they were."

Capturing her lips with mine, I divested her of the rest of her clothes, wrapping my arms around her body and bringing her down on the bed with me. Curving her under by body, my hands roamed taking extra time at her nipples, pulling and pinching.

To this she released me and gasped out for air, but I captured her lips once again needing to taste her again and again. I missed this. As fucked up as it was, I missed her.

Fuck. Since I'd left her, hadn't felt like fucking anyone, which was bizarre. Getting laid had never been a problem. Then having Carley suck me off did nothing.

This, though.

I was damn ready to go all fucking night.

Rylynn. Fuck me. She was heaven, somewhere I

never knew I'd have the pleasure of enjoying, but since I was there I would to the fullest.

Her hands roamed my body, nails scratching down my back as I fell between her legs and thrust inside of her in one deep penetration. The feel of her was even better than before. Slick, tight, and wet. The perfect pussy. She stilled, pulling away from my lips and arching her back with a moan as she stretched for me.

Knew I was a big man and gave her a moment to acclimate.

Lifting to my knees, I pulled her legs up with my forearms practically bending her in half, her pussy and ass up in the air perfect for the taking. Driving my cock down in her hard, screams fell from her lips and her eyes rolled into the back of her head as her hands gripped my biceps with so much force her nails drew blood. But I didn't give a fuck. Blood could be pouring out of me everywhere and I wouldn't stop. Couldn't stop.

My need for her was too great. It was too close to the surface, and there was no control left. Her sleek, wet pussy wrapped around me and clenched my cock over and over as she fell over the cliff calling out my name, her body spasming to the point of shaking. Her eyes closed as wave after wave of pleasure rocked her body.

Not waiting a single second, I pushed into the root, burying myself inside her and came hard. With each drop of my come entering her body, the tension in mine slowly began to melt away. Everything riding on my shoulders relaxed. Every problem that weighed on my mind disappeared. It was as if I were riding through the hills once again. Feeling free. Feeling at peace.

My weight fell down on her body, her arms going out to her sides, and I could feel her chest rising and falling with breaths. As her body shook, I took a few moments to bury my head in her neck inhaling her wild scent and putting it deep in my memory banks as a refresher. I swore her smell followed me when we parted before, but now having it fresh again, the craving for her magnified.

Wanting to stay buried inside of her, I flipped us so she was on top, my cock still inside semi-hard inside her and ready to go again. The relaxation of the orgasm was fantastic, but I needed to know that she was alright.

"Fucked you hard. You okay, Pixie?"

Her body shook with laughter, and I took that as a sign she didn't break because it was hard. "Great," she mumbled, lifting her head and resting her chin on my chest. "You know I would've come with you without all this pomp and circumstance."

"Pomp and circumstance?" I mimicked, amused.

"Yeah. All the drama back at the diner."

My brow quirked. "Sorry to tell ya, but you instigated that shit. Being all pissed off when I told you about not following that guy."

"Yep. And now that you bring it up, I'm still not over that shit."

Wrapping my arms tight around her, I said, "Too fucking bad."

"You're not my keeper."

This pissed me off. "Never said I was, but maybe you need one."

"Need one? Are you serious right now?"

Lifting up, my lips touched her briefly. "As a heart attack."

"I'll be sure to put that on my to-do list when I get back home."

This made me chuckle. "Next to batteries for your dildo."

Her hand came up and smacked her head. "I knew I forgot something. I have this one that has a suction cup on the end. I stick it on the wall and fuck myself with it."

My cock jumped still inside her, and she gasped. "Awe, did I stir up the bear?"

Fuck, the thought of watching her fuck herself on a huge cock with mine in her mouth was painful and made me want to run out and find a sex shop so that memory would be stuck in my head forever.

"You're slick already. Knew you'd be happy you came."

Her eyes rolled. "Really? You're the one who ordered me on your bike."

"You came."

"Like I had a choice."

I felt my chest get tight. "You always have a choice, but I knew in your eyes you wanted this just as fuckin' much as I did."

"I did."

"Then what the fuck?" I really wanted to know what the deal was here. We both got exactly what we wanted, even if she didn't want to admit it right then. I'd give her time to sort out her head while I fucked everything out of her.

"It's my job, Crow. You can't be pissed at that."

Cupping the back of her neck, her silky hair feathered through my fingers, another thing of hers that I missed. "Not pissed you're doin' your job. Pissed you don't have a man at your back during that shit. Pissed that this guy could be a sick fuck, find out you're tailin' him, and fuck you up. Pissed that your father or Cruz hasn't put a man on your back to do this shit."

She lifted a little higher and her eyes changed, expression becoming hard. The post-orgasm feeling sweeping clean away from her. "First, I'm not *yours* to worry about." I squeezed her hard, not liking the sound of this. Not liking her shutting me down one fucking bit. She continued, "Second, my father wanted a prospect to come with me when I first started, but since this isn't club business he understood my view of this."

"I have a very hard time thinking Rhys would just *understand* when it comes to his kid putting herself out there in any way, shape, or form."

She sucked in her bottom lip showing a slight vulnerability, but her shoulders lifted contradicting herself. "Look, it wasn't a good time. But we had it out and when he wouldn't let up I stopped telling anyone except two of my people what I was doing. It's worked out well so far."

In other words, she was keeping it from the club, and it pissed me off because Rhys was far from a stupid man. He had to know what the fuck was going on with his daughter. "I don't like it."

"And you have no say."

A growl rumbled up my chest again, not appreciating her trying to shut me out. No one shut me out, and Rylynn was going to learn that fact. "My cock inside you?"

She wiggled her ass. "Yep."

"That means I do."

"Nope. I'm not one of your whores in your club. You don't tell me what I can and can't do. *We* don't work like that. *We* fuck. That's it."

"Do ya wanna make a bet on that one?" I felt my anger rising, and my body tensed feeling it coming. I always had a say so, and with Rylynn a fucking bigger one that even I wasn't sure I wanted to admit yet. She would be safe, dammit. We didn't just fuck, and she knew it. She had to feel it too.

"Crow, let's just have fun tonight, and then I need to head back to Sumner. I've got other cases that need my attention. You helped me out, and I'm grateful for that. My cover at least isn't blown. But there's no need to make this any more than what it is. A fun time between two people."

The deep growl came up through my throat vibrating my chest, my hands gripping her tighter. Women leaving my bed had never been an issue before. Fuck them and out. That had been my way since high school. I'd had my fair share of pussy, but not a single one of those women drew me in like Rylynn did. Wanting her, craving her, and desiring her every fucking moment. Not even Sophia had done that, and I thought when I was young she'd be my wife one day, which never happened.

Women came and went.

Never. Not one time did I want to grab a woman, tie her to my bed, and fuck her brains out every single second of the day, not letting her come up for air the entire time. Rylynn though, I'd love to do exactly that, but I couldn't because only tomorrow was free since the next day was the run for Xavier and Marcus, and that couldn't be missed. Fuck really, I didn't have that time either way considering all the other shit polluting our lives that I should've gone back to Rebellion to take care of.

Between Rook's mess, Sophia's new man, trying to find stupid Berry, getting Jenny in rehab, and making sure my kid was safe the plate was overfilled.

Maybe if I could fuck her out of my system, everything would go back to normal. The craving for her would mellow and not be every second of the fucking day. That was what I hadn't realized while being back in Rebellion; Rylynn was always there under my skin just laying in wait to burst out. She was who I'd thought about before going to sleep and fuck me, that was a stark realization that hit me like a damn boulder.

Even without the time, I was going to make it. The phone was a powerful thing and it would get used a lot. "Tonight, tomorrow, and tomorrow night. Leave that next morning."

"What?" she asked, her breath catching at the end of the word. Her heart picked up rhythm against my chest as I felt the rapid thumps. She liked the idea.

"That time. Me and you in this bed. Only leavin' for food." And for me to handle business, but I left that part out.

"So, you want me to stay here so you can fuck me delirious?"

I smiled, thinking that was at the top of the goal list. "Fuck yeah."

Her body wiggled against mine, my cock twitching. "Told you, I have to work."

"And I told you, I want you here with me." The demand was clear. No wouldn't be an option. I had shit that needed to be done too and on high priority, but I was cutting out time for her, and she would for me as well.

Her eyes flared, that burn of independence and defiance shooting right to my cock. Fuck, everything she did made me hard enough to pound nails.

"And I want a money tree in my backyard to spring from the depths of Tinkerbell's ass; doesn't mean it's gonna happen." She slid me out, rolled off me, landing on her back and looking up at the ceiling, arm going over her forehead. "Why?"

"Why?" For some reason, I wanted to burst out laughing. She really needed the answer to this question? I'd thought it was pretty clear considering my cock lay heavy and hard on my abs. The fucking woman was gorgeous with an abundance of tits and ass. She had to know she was hot and I desired her.

She turned to her side resting her elbow into the bed and head on her hand. "Yeah, why? You could get anyone to fuck you, Crow. You sure as hell don't need me."

Grabbing Rylynn, she fit under me like she was meant to be there, every curve of hers complementing mine. My lips crashed on to hers, giving her a taste once again of the desire I had for her. Then I proceeded to show her exactly why I needed her. Come hell or high water, she wasn't leaving and if she tried, I'd tear the sheets into strips and tie her to the fucking bed.

***

"THIS IS SO GOOD," Rylynn moaned as strings of mozzarella cheese fell off the pizza, making a path from her lips to the food. She tried getting it all in her mouth, but there was too much and she needed her finger to help twirl it, then sucked it off. It was pizza foreplay and thoughts of me shoving the pizza box onto the floor and fucking her came directly to mind.

"Why is it I'm hard just from watching you eat?"

She shrugged, chewing, swallowing, then saying, "Because I'm a sexy bitch."

A chuckle escaped me. It was another thing that Rylynn gave me, the easy humor like we'd known each other for years instead of only weeks. Really only a couple of days. It was a challenge of getting one over on her and seeing her smile. It was just her. She was relaxed and comfortable in her own skin.

We'd fucked twice more before Rylynn claimed that if she didn't get food she was going to pass out, making some smartass comments about the queen needing sustenance making me laugh again. Since I wanted to have a marathon fucking night, we ordered food and had it delivered, but it was late.

Since my brothers and I found her before we could eat, I was pretty fucking starved too. So while we waited, I ate her. She was full of shit about not having energy because her hips moved in time with my lips, tongue, and teeth pulling another screaming orgasm out of her. All the while her taste filled my mouth. It was like an addiction.

"Yeah, Pixie. You are."

"Now that we're actually talking and you don't have your cock in some hole of mine, how have you been?"

Shoveling in my slice, chewing then swallowing, I answered, "Good, Pixie. Goin' day by day. You?"

She threw her crust into the box and picked up another slice. "Got three new cases I'm workin' on, and my sister thinks I can change my father's mind about her going to a friend's house. All in all steady." The pizza didn't have a chance as she took a huge bite. It was nice she didn't have an aversion to food. Some women only ate salads because they were afraid of not being skin and bones. Me, I'd always loved a woman. Rounded with tits and ass. Rylynn's food settled in all the right places on her, and I'd order as many pizzas as she wanted to keep her the way she was. She was confident in her body, sitting naked eating. Fuck, I liked that.

"How long have you been doing this?"

She swallowed, wiping her mouth with a tissue. "Since I was sixteen."

Food lodged in my throat at this declaration. "You're fuckin' shittin' me."

"Nah. It was little stuff like finding a friend's car that her parents ended up stealing because they found out she was at a party drunk with boys, or finding out who started some rumor, which ended up being the chick's best friend. She wanted her boyfriend. I didn't get into the good stuff that paid until I turned eighteen, but doing it early put my name out there. It helped."

"So you're what? Twenty-five, twenty-six?"

She laughed full out, tossing the pizza into the box and wiping her hands on the Kleenex we found in the room. "You really want the answer to this, Crow?"

I wasn't sure if this answer would change anything, but... "Well, you're not fuckin jailbait so yeah."

"I'm nineteen. I'll be twenty in a month."

My hand stilled, the slice of pizza beginning to droop down, but I was too stunned. She was closer to my son's age, not that it mattered, but she didn't act like she was that young. She had a maturity about her that spoke volumes. Maybe that was from growing up in this life and seeing what she saw and how things were. "What?"

"Nineteen, Crow."

"Fuck me."

"What, an old guy like you can't keep up?" she

joked, and my pizza was tossed into the box which was shoved off the bed. I tackled her while she giggled and laid my body on top of hers, smothering her with my heat.

Falling between her legs, there was no preamble. There was no touching. All there was, was my cock thrusting inside of her hard and fast. Her hands came up to touch me, and I pinned them down clasping our fingers together.

Her body shuddered under me as her neck arched giving me a beautiful view of her smooth neck. Not missing a beat with that invitation, my lips went to her throat kissing, nipping, sucking and feeling each of her breaths as I stirred her up.

She was on the cusp, and I pulled out only leaving the very tip of my cock inside of her. Her eyes shot up to mine. "Don't stop."

To this I smiled. "This old guy can't keep up, remember."

She glared. "Not funny, Crow. Fuck me already."

Slamming into her, I pulled back out only leaving the tip in once again.

"Asshole!" Rylynn yelled as she tried to fight for her hands to be freed, no doubt to scratch the shit out of me to get her way. Too bad that wasn't happening.

"You gotta problem with our ages?"

Her glare turned to ice. "That's it. Move off of me so I can finish myself off."

I didn't budge. "You're with me—my cock, fingers, or tongue are the only things inside of you."

She growled so deep it shook my chest. I liked this, keeping her on edge until I was ready to let her have it.

"Did you forget your Wheaties this morning? Not enough energy to finish the job?" She'd changed tactics on me going for smartass. Unlucky for her, I liked that part of her even more.

"Three big bowls. We're goin' all night."

My hips moved up just a touch pressing inside her, then retreated. Fuck, it was torture for me not to slip balls deep inside of her, but I had something to prove.

She wiggled her hips trying to get me further in, but I didn't allow that. "What do you want?" This was on a shout of utter frustration. A light sheen of sweat glistened off her forehead.

"Answer my question."

"What was that again? I mean, I have a cock inside of me and an orgasm only a thrust away."

Another chuckle escaped. "Why am I laughing while fucking you?"

"Don't know, but you're not fucking me," she retorted.

"Do you have an issue with our ages?"

"Fuck no." The declaration came out fierce and immediate. She was telling the truth. "Now fuck me with that big cock of yours."

I continued with the short movements keeping her

right there on the edge ready to tumble over into the abyss of pleasure. Saying nothing, I just stared down into her green eyes that right now looked like a dragon about to breathe fire.

Fuck, something else to turn me on with.

"What? Did you want something?" Like there needed to be one more thing.

The noise from her lips was low and guttural as she bucked her hips trying to get me off. Too bad for her I weighed probably double what she did. There was no way she'd get what she wanted.

"You really are a dick. Maybe you should put a condom over your head."

My head flew back as I laughed all the while she struggled, not liking this one bit. Her words, though. Condom. Fuck. The realization hit, I hadn't used a single one with Rylynn. Actually, anytime I'd been inside of her, I hadn't gloved up.

My first kid came from being young and stupid not using protection. I learned my lesson and gloved up every time after that. Still had no fucking idea how Jenny got pregnant. My luck she put holes in the rubbers. After the test said Van was mine it was too late, and I wouldn't trade anything for my baby girl.

But Rylynn. Fuck.

"Pixie." Her eyes blazed up. "Haven't used a condom." I watched her expressions trying to take her pulse on this fact. She gave nothing away. "You on the pill?"

Her jaw got hard, then relaxed. "I have an IUD. You clean?"

"Always wrap up. Last time tested clean."

"Fuck." Her arms went slack and body relaxed, catching me off guard.

"What?"

Her eyes rolled up to the ceiling. "Bet you say that to all the girls."

Releasing her fingers, I cupped her face until she was looking directly at me and pushed in all the way to the root, connecting us in every way possible. She groaned, and I waited for her eyes to come to mine. This was serious, and she needed to know I wasn't fucking around.

"No. I glove up and get tested. No way I'm goin' out due to some kind of STD."

"You didn't with me."

"No, I didn't. You're different."

She let out a large puff of air, and I thought for sure she was going to come back with something smartass about me telling all the women that she was *different* and I was going to have to spank her ass, but she surprised me by saying, "I believe you."

That left part of my chest warmed as I began to move my hips. Her hands came to my neck, while mine kept her face on me. Close. Connected. One. Fuck, it was nice.

Her face went soft as she didn't take her gaze off me. There was something big happening here. The connection between us was so damn strong, there felt like this pull to her like no other. She was burrowing herself deeper inside of me every second we spent together.

Leaning down, I gave her a soft kiss, my hips still moving in and out. Her hands gripped my neck tighter. Fuck, that felt good.

"I'm going to come," she whispered so softly.

"Eyes on me," I ordered, swirling my hips. This set her off as she flew, her eyes never leaving mine. This took effort because she wanted to close them so damn bad, but she forced them to stay wide open. She allowed me to see the beauty that was Rylynn. Her passion and heart. Everything right there on the surface ready to be held close. Begging me to take a hold and never let her go. Jesus.

"Beautiful," I whispered, leaning down to kiss her softly continuing to move as I felt mine coming. This wasn't hard or fast. It was slow and intense. I'd fucked her every time we'd been together. This wasn't that, nowhere close. She was a burr that kept going deeper and deeper in my skin, making a home there not wanting to leave.

As I came, my eyes never left her soft, sated ones.

We built a bridge in that moment. One that was sturdy with the beginnings of a strong foundation to continue to grow, expand, and see where it would take us.

We had a day to see if what was between her and I was a fluke or something real on both sides of the coin. I needed to use my time wisely.

13

Rylynn

A PHONE RANG WAKING ME FROM A DEEP SLUMBER. Sunlight poured in through the large crack in the curtains that we failed to close up tight before we passed out. Not that either of us would've attempted to move, because we couldn't. The man sure as hell knew what he was doing.

The clock said ten forty-five, meaning we only had four hours of sleep. My body felt it.

"Crow," he answered as I closed my eyes trying to chase sleep once again. It was right there on the cusp and only part of me was able to make it. The other part wouldn't shut the hell up.

Crow had fucked me so many times during the night parts of my body throbbed because they hadn't ever been used so much. I was completely worn out and happily sated. Happy, content, at peace—all these emotions I hadn't felt since before losing my grandpa. This was a solace for some reason I could only find with Crow. It wasn't just the sex that did it, though. He made me smile and gave a shit what I did in my life. Sure, he didn't like me tailing men, but that didn't mean I'd ever stop.

Shaking my head to clean out my thoughts, I focused on the sex because that was all this could be, and getting emotions involved was stupid as hell with a man like Crow. It was a setup for shit things to happen. Like I didn't know a broken heart. Because that was where I was headed if these thoughts didn't shut the fuck up.

Crow knew exactly how to bring every bit of pleasure out of me. Sometimes it paid to have an older, experienced man to really make your body sing.

Out of all the times we fucked, there was once when it was something more. I felt like it was a dangerous game I was playing letting myself read into things, but I wasn't one to look for more. I felt it, though. The time when he told me not to look away from him as I came and he did the same. No, that time he'd made love to me. There was a huge difference from every other time, and I felt it in every way possible.

While we stared in each other's eyes finding our releases, my heart squeezed and tears threatened to escape, but I held them in. Barely.

There was definitely something between the two of us. Not only were we combustible, there was deep feeling there as well. One that excited me and scared the shit out of me at the same time. *Sex, Rylynn. Pull your head out of your ass. You know better than this.*

"Bring me Rylynn's keys and head home. Prepare and I'll meet you tomorrow before."

Cryptic words that didn't take a rocket scientist with a fancy degree hanging on the wall to figure out. Whatever their business was, it was here not in Rebellion. That was why he had time to stay, because his brothers would be back and he'd meet up with them then. Sometimes it was scary how well I knew this life.

"Right," he said then told whoever was on the phone where we were and gave them our room number. "Later," he called out, and I heard the phone clatter on the side table.

Strong arms pulled me against a hard, warm body. His hand started playing with my nipple, swirling around the tip so feather light, then pulling. I groaned. "Crow... I need to sleep." It was true, but my body was ready to get up and join the show.

"You can sleep when you're dead." His hand skated down between my legs giving my clit a roll and a glide, waking my body up once again. Traitorous bitch!

"Fine. But you're doin' the work and then I sleep."

"Done," he decreed and proceeded to show me

exactly why sleeping when you're dead was a good way to go.

MY PHONE RANG with the tone I gave all my clients so I could tell who was calling, just from the ring. There were three family and friends or something to do with work. It was simple. The well-defined arm around me tightened as I reached over to the nightstand, grabbing my phone and seeing the name Cindy, the woman whose husband I lost last night. Double shit.

I'm sorry. I wanted to get laid so following your husband took a back seat to an alpha male with a solid body that makes me scream and body sing. Therefore, what you're paying me to do doesn't matter.

Umm. No.

"Hello."

"Rylynn. What did you find?"

Letting out a sigh, I wiggled my ass into Crow trying to get him to let me go, but it backfired as his hand snaked around my hip to my stomach. I clenched my legs together tight, and I could feel his body shake from laughter. Damn man knew what I wanted, but he had other ideas.

Unable to tell him to take a long jump off a short pier, I had to answer Cindy. "Absolutely nothing, Cindy. He went directly to the hotel alone, went to the office, went to dinner on his own. There was no other woman."

"I just don't believe that. Did he go back to the hotel after dinner?"

Since I didn't know exactly if he pulled off the side of the road and grabbed a hooker on the way, which I highly doubted, he was that boring. I answered, "Yep. Found nothing, Cindy, at all."

"Really?"

"Wouldn't lie to ya."

Her long exhale came through the line. "Okay, can you send the bill to me at work. I can email you the address."

"That mean you want to close it out?"

"For now. We're having a really tight month, but I needed to know. Thank you." Relief swarmed me like a thousand butterflies. Not only would I be paid, there was no going after him again. Bonus was fucking Crow all night. A win-win in my book. Guess coming here ended up being exactly what I needed.

"Any time."

"Well, I hope never again. I'll email you the address," she retorted, and I couldn't blame her one bit.

"Will do."

"Thanks." Before I could reply the line discon-nected. Crow's face was nuzzling the back of my neck through my hair. Why did this man have to be so damn hot? Every damn move he made turned me on like no other. He breathed and my pussy clenched. Why? It wasn't fair for the rest of the male population. Maybe he should look into being cloned. Food for thought.

"You're done with that case?" he said through kisses sending goose bumps up my arms.

My breaths began to grow more rapid. "Yeah. One down, two to go."

He didn't stop at my neck. It was like he needed to mark every inch of my skin with his scent. "What are they?"

My body was responding to him, my hips beginning to circle feeling his cock harden. My mind was having a hard time keeping up because the sensations were becoming intense.

"What?"

He chuckled, his hand moving down my stomach. "Your cases. What else do you have?"

"Man cheating on his wife liking pony play from another man and a missing persons case." I groaned, back arching and temperature spiking. It didn't occur to me until much later that I just gave him that. Telling him with no qualms about it whatsoever. It just came out. Only two people knew, now there were three.

Crow flipped around and pulled me on top of him, my pussy feeling very empty all of a sudden and demanding it be filled. Wiggling down, the tip of him just crest my entrance, but his arms around my waist halted my descent.

"What?" I snipped, needing his cock inside me— now. We were not going to do this whole tease Rylynn until she wants to kill him thing again.

"Pony play?"

My hair fell in a sheet around us as I stared down at him. "Yeah, now will you fuck me already?"

"Was it hot?"

The thought of it made a small bit of my arousal disappear. Not that I wasn't adventurous, just never with ponies. "No, and if you don't stop talking about it, my desire to fuck you is going to evaporate in a puff of smoke."

With one tip of his hips and his arms pulling me down, he impaled me. A cry escaped. Even after having him so many damn times, he still stretched me each time. Damn it was hot. I could feel every inch of his cock and the best part was when he was about to come, because I could feel every single drop of his come. It was sexy as hell.

He held me still, unable to get the friction I so desperately needed to come. Glaring down at him, I ordered, "Move, Crow!"

"What's with this missing person case?" he asked, and I wasn't following along, my brain in orgasm mode instead of talking about shit that didn't need to be discussed mode. My head fell to his forehead. He was so frustrating.

"Girl. Cops don't have any other leads, her parents are desperate to find her. Now, will you move?!" The last part came out on a shriek as my core clenched needing more. More of his cock, more movement, or more friction. I didn't give a shit which, but something had to give.

He thrust twice and stopped. Yes, twice. What the ever-loving fuck! "Any other cases?"

I shook my head learning quickly that this was his way of getting information out of me and I needed to think, but he made it difficult. "Not at the moment. Now can we do this?"

Crow didn't release me, but instead placed his feet on the bed and his hips began to pound up inside me over and over like a jackrabbit on crack. His cock hit so deep inside me, to that special place that I swore with him was another G-spot.

I couldn't move. All I could do was take. And take. And take. When we both found it, my head crashed to his shoulder as I tried to breathe. It was a very difficult task. "You're trying to kill me."

"Death by sex—who wouldn't want that to be the way they go."

A smile tipped my lips. "Now who's the smartass."

A hard slap came to my left ass cheek as I tried to jump yelling out some choice words, but he didn't allow it. It was coming to my understanding that this man didn't do anything he didn't want to, and he got off on making others do as they were told, at least in the bedroom.

Scary thing was, I loved it too. Loved that he took control. That I didn't have to think if I was doing something he didn't like. He made sure to make it so he did and the same with me. The way he watched me, learning what made me moan in different ways was such a damn turn on.

I was falling hard, which was a terrible thing. Lord help me.

14

Rylynn

"GET ON," CROW ORDERED AS I SWUNG MY LEG OVER HIS bike, my Jeep parked next to it in the hotel lot. The husband's car was long gone considering it was coming upon dusk and was due to leave early that morning. My stomach growled, and I did as told. Hunger could make a woman do just about anything, at least for me.

I loved my food. Thanksgiving was my favorite holiday. The day when you get together with your friends and family, stuff yourself full of all the goodness and pass out in a food induced coma. Who wouldn't want that?

Crow drove for a while. The ride smooth, my arms around him holding him tight. Each mile that passed my body melted more and more into him. He pulled into a chain restaurant sit-down place and parked the bike. I just stopped myself from telling me to forget food and just ride.

Getting off we walked in and were seated immediately into a booth. Crow slid in with ease as if his body just moved on its own. Stealthy like a panther, slick, smooth. How could something like sliding into a booth be so damn hot? It's not supposed to be, but him, hell he breathes and I could have a spontaneous orgasm.

We both ordered, and the waitress brought our drinks.

"Pixie?" he asked, grabbing my attention from the stupid paper that comes from the straws they set on the table for your drinks. I'd always had a thing with fidgeting with them, twisting and turning to see what I could make. The damn things were addicting, just like the man across from me.

My eyes lifted, seeing his sympathetic. "Yeah."

"I'm sorry about Dagger."

My heart stopped momentarily. That was not expected in the slightest, and I felt it all the way to my bones. That pain slicing through me once again leaving yet another fresh wound for me to bleed out from.

Even knowing the asshole who did it was gone didn't lessen the hurt.

He reached out and grabbed my hands allowing me to feel his warmth and gather strength from him. That felt damn good to have someone other than myself to carry the burden even if it was for a short time.

"I am too." His death was so damn raw, but I imagined that wouldn't end anytime soon unfortunately. Everyone grieves differently, and I was still trying to find my path with dealing and understanding everything that had happened. The pain of losing him sat deep in my soul, and I had no idea how to help myself except what I'd been doing, keeping on keeping on. Every day was a new one, and the only time I didn't feel that burn of grief was inside Crow's arms.

He gave my hands a reassuring squeeze and asked, "So your sister thinks you can change your father's mind about something?"

Relief hit that he was changing the subject. It wasn't that I didn't like talking about my grandpa. Remembering him was important. It was the fact that learning to cope was difficult, and a lot and the answers weren't all there yet.

I explained Mazie's predicament to his smile. Loved that I could put that look on his face.

"You have a bike?" he asked, deeply interested.

"Out of all I just said, you latched on to me having a bike?" Such a man.

He let go of my hands and leaned back in his seat. My hands felt cold instantly, and I put them in my lap to try to warm them up, but it didn't work as well without his.

My head shook, and a smile tipped my lips. "Yeah. My dad and I worked on it for months. We started when I turned sixteen. He found an old beat-up piece of shit that needed work from top to tail. By the time I was seventeen and able to get my motorcycle license, it was done and I was able to use my bike for the test."

"Really?"

A smile creeped in. "Yeah. My dad appreciates hard work and dedication to something. That was what I showed him with this project. I loved it because I got to spend time with him."

"So how did you round up bad guys if you were working on a bike?"

Our food arrived at the table. Patty melt for me and burger for him. I reached over grabbing the ketchup and putting a huge blob on my plate to dip my fries in.

"Back then, that was just small stuff and it wasn't like I had people banging down my door to see if Cindy Lou Who stole Betty's boyfriend. Therefore, I worked around it, learning as each day passed."

"You do realize you're the shit," he said, surprising me so much I almost choked on a fry.

I coughed, patting my chest as I waved off the waitress who thought I was choking. I kind of was, but whatever. His comment knocked me on my ass in a bizarre way.

Getting my throat cleared I responded, "Oh yeah?"

"Yep. You are. And what I say goes, so deal with it."

I laughed. "I know I'm the queen of my castle."

He set his burger down and leaned back. "Oh hell. Are you into that fairytale bullshit?"

My head shook, and I got a handle on the coughs. "No. I'm not some damsel in distress who needs to be rescued by some fucked up prince whose nails are crystal clean. A man needs to keep up with what I do and deal with my job, my family, and my life. If he doesn't, he's out. So far, haven't found a man who fits those categories."

Crow didn't touch that and asked, "You grew up in the club, right?"

Dunking a fry in ketchup, I nodded.

"Then I take it you like this life. All it entails."

I swallowed and answered immediately, "Love it. It's all I know, Crow. My family is the most important thing to me. I didn't just grow up with my father. There was an entire club that were honorary uncles. Each one of those men would have stood up for me, beat anyone's ass that fucked with me, and were my family. Family isn't always blood. It's having those around you who give a shit. Me, I was lucky to have my parents, both involved. But I also had every guy in that club at the ready. And I have to say that it wasn't always the greatest to have them all in my business. The first date I ever went on alone had to meet me at the clubhouse. Having big, bad bikers standing around me, armed and threatening, my date almost took off. Personally, I wished he just would've. He was a pussy." Curiosity hit me at his line of questioning, and my attention became even more acute. "Why?"

He shook his head, but answered. "Just tryin' to get to know ya."

This seemed fair and really nice, so I gave him more. "My parents 'story is all kinds of crazy. The nuts and bolts are that my mom, Tanner, killed a man who beat the shit her mom, my grandma, Mearna. They went to Ravage for safety because grandma knew Dagger wouldn't turn her away. They'd loved each other for years, but spent it apart because she didn't want to live the club life. He didn't know anything about my mom and that was a rocky road, but it brought my mom and dad together. My dad says he took one look at my mom and just knew she was the one for him. The rest is history."

"Knew she was it huh?" He took a bite of his burger and began chewing, listening to me with avid fascination. It made me wonder what he thought of all of it. He'd no doubt seen some crazy shit in his lifetime; a little murder wouldn't turn him off in the slightest.

"Yeah. With Dad being my grandpa's best friend, it got tricky at first, but my dad didn't give that first shit about any of it. He wanted my mom and claimed it immediately. My grandpa knew it and didn't push." I stopped taking a bite of my patty melt and washed it down with a diet. "Dad doesn't talk much about it, but my mom told me all the details. I think she didn't want me to go down the same path as her."

"What, killing someone?"

This I felt in my gut and shook my head. "No. Living with regret and having the power to change it. My mom missed over twenty years with my grandpa because her mom didn't want to raise her daughter in the club. That time lost hit her really hard once she found out back then. When Grandpa died, it opened a wound for her that never quite healed. There was so much time lost, and that's the one thing in this life you can never get back. My grandma feels it too. The guilt of keeping father and daughter apart. She's told me before that it kills her to even think about."

He wiped his mouth with the napkin swiping off some mayo. "Yeah, that had to be hard on everyone's end."

"Yeah. I couldn't imagine not knowing who my dad is. I mean, he's not the easiest man to deal with, but his heart is solid for his family. Always knew that. Never once in my life had he ever proved me wrong on that. Even when I got in trouble and he was furious with me, I knew he'd never really hurt me, but if anyone else besides me saw his face, they'd be scared shitless and piss their pants."

I sucked back some more diet setting the glass back to the table.

"So smartass little you got in trouble, huh? That I

just can't see one bit," he mocked, and the urge to kick him under the table hit hard, but I held it back.

"Look, my dad now knows I'm the queen and can do no wrong, so it's all good."

He chuckled. Damn, I loved that sound. "Now that I don't believe for a second. You may be the princess, but your momma is the queen in your old man's eyes."

He was right, but instead of agreeing I said, "I'm the queen of my own castle. I live my life on my own. Love my parents with everything inside of me, but I'm my own woman. Mom made sure of that. We fight, but that's normal. Overall, we have a really good relationship. The good times outweigh the bad, who could ask for better? What about you? Your mom and dad around?"

Crow finished chewing his bite then sucked back some Coke. "Mom's not around. Hasn't been since I was little and don't give much shit about her. She fucks with my dad which pisses me off, but she steers clear of me."

The gasp came quickly and I tried to shut it down, but it didn't work. "Sorry."

He shrugged. "It's the same as you. I don't know any different. My dad is my rock, been there through everything, and he gave me all the brothers of the club from the time I was born. They all meant a lot to me before I earned my cut. They were family from the very beginning." He swiped his lips with his thumb. "My dad though, he's sick with prostate cancer, but he says the treatment he's under right now is working, so we're rolling with it in hopes he pulls through it."

"I can tell you love him."

"Yep," was all he answered before finishing off his burger.

"Life loves to throw shit at us over and over again challenging us throughout our years. We just have to learn to either duck when it flies or beat the shit out of it."

He smirked. "Let me guess, you'd beat the shit out of it?"

I swiped my mouth pushing my plate to the center of the table. "Absolutely."

"Come on, let's get out of here. That's enough of the heavy for now."

That night would go down in history as the time when I really let a man into my life, explaining about my family. Opening myself up to him at my core and allowing him access into parts I'd never shared with another man before, and I didn't regret a single second of it. It was also a night I would never forget until I took my last breath.

THE BRIGHT SUNLIGHT filled me with dread. It was supposed to be happy and make you feel good. All the vitamins or whatever that makes a person high on life. Not today, though. Today I felt dread crawling all over me like spiders. It was uncommon for me, and I didn't like the feeling. Unfortunately, there was no other choice.

He needed to get to his club in Alabama. While I needed to go the opposite way to Sumner and get shit going on the missing girl. I'd read everything there was and needed to get out there and see what I could find.

But I didn't want to leave this bubble of ours we'd created. It had been fun, intriguing, and eye opening learning more about Crow and his life. If only we lived closer to one another, maybe we could give this a go and see where it would lead us. That wasn't in the cards, though.

Sucked, but we had responsibilities. Damn life.

If this was going to be our last hurrah together, I was going to make it so he never forgot me. I wanted to be burned on his soul so he took me everywhere he went and held me close forever. So any woman who came after me would know that part of him was mine, and I'd never give it up. It would be held so close to him that nothing would penetrate it.

Sliding down his body, he began to stir, but before he did fully I engulfed his semi-hard cock into my mouth and down my throat. My gag reflex was nonexistent, and I had no clue why. It had always been that way allowing me to throw back some serious liquor.

Judging from the jolt of his body, Crow liked it a hell of a lot.

His fingers laced through my hair as my head and hand worked double time. My hand massaging his balls while my mouth did the rest. I may not have had the gag reflex, but opening my mouth wide enough to get around him was a bit of a challenge as he got harder and harder. Damn man had to be as round as a fucking Coke can.

"Pixie," he groaned, his grip getting tighter, pulling. I loved the feel of it so much wetness pooled between my legs. Getting him off was getting me off. The way it should be when you're with a man.

I kept repeating the up and down thrusts over and over again, the veins becoming more pronounced. Licking the underside of his dick, he grabbed me under my armpits, picked me up, and set me down on his cock. That was hot. Like only saw it in the movies hot, and he could do it as many times as he wanted considering the wetness between my legs started to run down my thigh.

"Ride me," he ordered, and I did, losing control of myself, grinding down, swirling my hips right then left. My clit kept pulsing with each motion, and my thrusts down started to become ragged because I couldn't control my body. It moved whatever way it could to reach its height. It was ready to explode around him. Just needed a little bit more.

Crow knifed up so I was sitting on his lap, his cock inside of me. "Eyes," he told me, and I complied wrapping my limbs around him, my body screaming to release. Once we were connected, my orgasm hit with a vengeance as Crow's arms tightened around me pulling me closer to him. His cock twitched inside of me telling me he released.

We didn't lose contact for a long while. We sat in that position, neither of us wanting to move and break this connection. I felt my heart tear like a rip in thin paper scoring all the way through. It was stupid and insane, but there it was burning inside of me knowing this was really and truly over.

There would be no reason for our paths to cross again. It was by coincidence this time happened. And wasn't that depressing as shit.

He felt it too. I could tell looking deep into his eyes. This connection was beautiful and killed at the same time. Knowing we would never have it. I refused to cry even though it lodged in my throat.

Crow had the control to break the moment by kissing my lips, pulling out and laying me next to him, tucking me close. He just held me trailing his fingertips over my hip. Each touch sent shocks down my frame so soft and tender coming from a man who was anything but. Something else to burn into my memory. This sated, content happy, yet unbelievable painful memory.

We stayed like this until it was time we had to leave, neither of us speaking just allowing our bodies to do it for us. Both of us getting lost as the seconds ticked by.

It sucked this had to be the end of the road, but life wasn't fair and not everything worked out the way you'd hoped it would. Most of the time it never did. Life was a mean bitch and when she slapped you in the face, you felt the sting for a long damn time.

We dressed and left the hotel. Each step we took was another toward losing each other forever.

Crow pressed me against my Jeep and brought his lips down to mine. The kiss was bruising and hard turning me on all over again. It was also painful, not physically, but emotionally. A good-bye that never should happen, but it was.

He never said a word about his comment about 'me being on the back of his bike' and I never brought it up in our time together, not wanting to bring anymore of the heavy into our time together. Since he never said anything either, it didn't have the same meaning as I'd thought. Until that moment I hadn't realized how much I wanted that for us so we could explore this and see what another day would bring.

Alas, it wasn't the right time for us. Maybe in another life or another way, but not in this one.

We took the chance saying with our bodies what couldn't be said with words. Neither one of us promised the other anything but a good time. It was uncomplicated, freeing, but I already regretted leaving him and he was right in front of me, in my space and that regret burned.

This track of thinking wasn't helping him or myself. I needed to let it go.

He lifted his head from mine. "Phone."

I was in a fog from his kiss and only got out a whispered, "What?"

"Give me your phone."

My head shook trying to gather my thoughts, my hair flying back and forth. "Why?"

He held out his hand and I rolled my eyes, digging in my bag and pulling it out. He didn't move a damn inch to help me out with this process. Instead, he stayed plastered to me, his cock hard against my belly. Lord. It was good we were going our different ways. He really was going to kill me by sex.

Handing it over, he tried to open it, but it was locked. He lifted his brow at me, and I smiled. "What? Need something?"

"Unlock it."

"You're awfully demanding. Did someone piss in your Cheerios this morning?"

He growled low, "You know damn well I ate you for breakfast."

A chuckle escaped me at remembering that meal right before we got dressed as I held out my hand. Hell if I knew what he was doing, but there was a small glimmer of hope that he wanted to stay connected to me.

I pressed my index finger to the back of the phone, and it unlocked. Crow snatched it back right away looking down at it and swiping his finger this way and that.

He punched in some numbers and a phone rang then stopped as he handed my phone back to me. "Now I have your number. You have mine. You call me when you get home."

"I don't..." I began, wanting this but fearing it in the same breath. Would I love to hear his voice over the phone, yes. My concern though was would it be enough.

He interrupted me by touching his nose with mine, his eyes boring into mine shutting my mouth. "Call me. If you don't, I'm riding to Sumner."

"That's stupid, Crow. I'm a big girl..."

He cut me off again. "Know that, but that doesn't mean I have to like this shit. You get home, you call me."

I nipped the tip of his nose. "Fine. You really need to take a Xanax."

"No, what I need is to lock you up in my room and not let you out."

This made my body tingle. "Yum... That sounds like a great idea. Promise?"

He shook his head probably trying not to throttle

me so I just smiled at him, loving this back and forth. He challenged me, tempted me, and tore at me, each one I loved. That push and pull was something to seriously get off on.

"Rylynn, I have to go and meet my brothers. You need to get home." He leaned down kissing me hard, once again stealing my breath. He released me all too soon and took a step back. That one step becoming miles between us. "Get in and go."

Immediately my mind said, *no, just stay, get on the back of his bike and ride.* My body was on the same page with my mind, but he didn't ask me to do that. Crow wasn't and would never be mine to stay with and be with. He had a life as did I. We were too far apart. Our time together was fun, and as much as it killed I needed to leave it at that and be done.

What in the hell was wrong with me? *This was fun, Rylynn. Nothing else. No matter what you felt at the time, it needed to be washed away.*

"Bye, Crow." The croak in my throat made me give a slight cough and the damn tears I'd been able to hold back threatened to come back full force. Damn emotions. They always seemed to make their presence known at the most inopportune times.

Opening the door and using every bit of strength ingrained in me over the years, I got in to hear him say, "Later, Pixie."

Later. Later was going to be a long fucking time.

More like forever. As I pulled away and headed home, I'd realized part of me left with Crow that day and was now traveling away from me. A part that was for now and would always be only his.

When my mother told me the stories of her and my father, I knew one day it would hit me like it hit my father. I'd see the one and it would smack me in the face. Not everyone got their one, though. Guess it was my time to let go of one and find two. If there was one. I could hear my grandpa's voice in my head. *"No man is good enough for my little girl."* He'd then rub the top of my head. Too bad that would never be.

Why everything had to be so damn difficult, I'd never know. Day by day. Minute by minute. Second by second. My mom was right—living with regret was harsh, but when the feelings weren't mutual, it killed.

The pain of the knife to the heart was cut the deepest and was felt the most.

15

Crow

"You look way too fuckin' happy," Phoenix groused as I pulled up to the Chattanooga River cutting my engine, unable to stop grinning.

Being with Rylynn was a high no drug or ride on my bike could compare to. For a brief time, my mind was able to shut off. The contingency plans, different case scenarios, my kids, their mothers, my father—all of it I was able to shut down and just be with her in that moment. Be with her and actually feel. Something I hadn't done since Sophia back in high school. Rylynn was a fantastic lay. Never had better. Ever. No one even compared to her, but it wasn't just the sex. It wasn't. I knew it then and still knew it now.

"Yep," was all I answered.

"Where is she?" Brewer asked, standing next to me as we walked down the way to where we were picking up the shipment. Tall trees covered around a path large enough for our box truck to fit through to pick up the cargo. The shade helped stave off the heat.

"On her way home."

"You do realize her father will cut your balls off."

This came to my mind several times when Ry talked about her parents. They were good people, and there was no doubt in my mind her father would have a problem with us together considering how old I was to his little girl.

Knowing how her father was though, and the type of man I'd become, we'd figure it out. Fuck. I'd never be able to find out though if my theory was correct. She went her way, and I went mine. Didn't mean it felt good.

I stopped walking and turned my head just a touch to him. "He and I speak the same language."

Brewer's eyebrows rose as he crossed his hands over his chest. "Is it done?"

"What are you, my counselor now? Giving relationship advice?"

"Nope, just give a fuck."

I started walking once again moving to a small clearing. Our load should be coming down the river in twenty minutes, and playing a thousand questions about what happened with Rylynn wasn't on the top of my agenda to spend the time. It was no one's business but ours. "Preciate that, but don't need that shit and you know it."

"Always got your back, brother."

I nodded because he always would. "Enough of that shit. Talk to me."

He didn't hesitate as we climbed up an old picnic table sitting our asses down. It wasn't big enough so some stood around us. "Got a call this morning they were on their way. Load was full and ready for the truck. Drop off point has been scoped out, Ethan and Jimmy are there keeping tabs. Checked in with them when we got here, and everything was a go. The ride's about two and a half hours to the drop off; we're all gassed up and ready to roll."

Placing my elbows on the table, I asked, "No bad feelings about these guys?"

"Everything else pans out."

This was good. We needed this shit to go smooth for both of our ends. We needed to be able to trust Xavier and Marcus, and they needed to trust us. This world we lived in could be tipped at any time. All it would take was a single wrong move for everything to topple over. We'd gotten along well so far, but with the question of change I had my doubts, but that was my job. To be one step ahead. They paid us a shit load of cake for this run; hopefully it all worked out.

"Brief me on everything." In the hotel room, Rylynn didn't say a word when my phone rang and I had to take calls. Once she even went into the bathroom until I got off. Another time, she actually fell asleep. She was made for this life, cut from the same cloth. My head needed to not be on her and on the situations with the club.

The recaps over our phone calls were short though, only relaying bits and pieces to me. Therefore, I needed the full story before the shipment came in.

Tex started first. "Stephanie's healin' up. Bear had a chat with Goldi. Said it wasn't pretty, but she gets it. Goldilocks is even going as far as to run more checks on the clients we already have in the database just to make sure. She and I have talked to the girls, and they're good. One fucked up time didn't break their faith in us. Business is as usual."

"Berry?" I asked.

"Nothing with the cash. In looking through the credit card shit you took pictures of, there was only one place that stood out. The Purple Pride," Wrong Way started. "Before leaving his wife, he was there several times, but the charges weren't much. More like drinks or food. When we get back, we need to look into it."

"Good. Top of the list." I nodded to Wrong Way then turned to Lemon. "Lemon, what do you have for me?" He didn't exactly fidget, but there was a splash of uncertainty and I didn't fucking like that. His shit was slowly unraveling. The fucked up part of it was all he had to do was say he needed help and the club would do everything in our power to help. Instead, he continued to drown himself each and every day. He wasn't going to like the consequences of this.

"Did what you said about Jenny and her man. He's in to drugs and gambling. She's just doin' the drugs. No jobs to speak of, but they're in debt up to his eyeballs with Ebony."

"How deep?"

"Forty-seven thousand two hundred and twenty-two dollars."

A low whistle came from my lips because all that shit was now on Jenny's head. "And the house?"

"If Ebony has it or thinks she has it, I have no clue. Tried getting into her computer system, but it's tied tight." Fuck, he needed to be able to hack. With that option out, I turned to Phoenix.

"Phoenix, call Ebony and find out all you can about this shit. I want to know if the morons put the house up and for how much. She doesn't tell you, see if you can fuck it out of her."

Phoenix said nothing, just pulled out his phone taking a few steps off to the side. My gut was telling me this wouldn't be as easy as telling her the house was ours. "Next."

"Nothin' on who's tailin' us. I'd be surprised if there really is one at this point," Wrong Way said. "Even watchin' everything we do, nothin'. Jimmy went through all the tapes and saw nothin' out of the ordinary. Do you really think this is happening?"

"We do until we don't. Someone added those cameras. Step ahead, my man."

He nodded and looked to Lemon. "Can you get into the street cameras?"

"I can try."

"Try? Are you fuckin' shittin' me?" I barked.

He shook his head, his back straightening. "I'll get it." My faith in him was waning. Men were prideful, and I got that more than most. But if a man couldn't do his job, it was his balls to pick up off the floor and speak up for it.

"Wrong Way, work on this."

Wrong Way lifted his chin in response. Lemon was working my last fucking nerve. "Been training Ethan on the computer." This had my head lifting to Wrong Way. "He's fuckin' good. Smart. Knows new shit that's out there. You want him on this with me?"

"He's not patched."

"He needs to be," Wrong Way replied. A ringing endorsement from the man who didn't give those out freely. It was time to bring the man into the fold.

"Next church we'll vote. Now. Need you on it."

"Got it," Wrong Way replied as I looked over to Lemon. His face was red with fury. Good, maybe that would get the stick out of his ass and get him working harder. Sometimes a man needed a kick in the ass to get his act together. Other times, he failed. I hoped to Christ Lemon could pull his head out.

A few moments later a very large boat was spotted coming down the river as we all came to attention, guns coming out and at our sides.

The boat had two floors and looked like it should be in the ocean with some rich muckety-mucks laying on top of it out in the sun. It absolutely did not look like a boat that should be riding down the Chattanooga River for a stroll. This was a huge red flag to anyone around us.

Stupid. These fuckers were stupid.

I hated stupid people, and these motherfuckers were getting off on the wrong foot straightaway. It only took one time for them to fuck up to a point we'd cut them off. This might just be that time.

The boat slowly pulled up to the dock. A man with a shaved head lifted his chin at us as he docked the boat. It wasn't an actual dock, just a concrete pole that was used to tie off boats. It had been there for years, but was strong as hell.

Bald guy did it quickly and efficiently, like he'd done this several times before. Something positive.

"Word," Brewer said, moving up to the guy.

The bald man didn't hesitate or flinch that Brewer had his gun out ready to put a bullet in his head. "Dick sucker." We always had a code word or phrase to make sure we were getting what we needed to and when. My father used to do it before me as well. It had never steered us wrong. For this one several of my brothers chuckled. Lately the code words were becoming a form of entertainment.

"You got it?" Brewer asked.

Dick sucker guy nodded. "Yeah. Need help gettin' it out."

"Phoenix, Rooster, and Hornet, go check it out." They broke off, boarding the boat while dick sucker didn't even flinch, keeping his stare on me. It only took moments and the guys were back up from the bottom of the boat.

"It's there."

I nodded over to Wrong Way and he took off to get the truck, backing it up for easy transfer. The place we did this we knew well. Had been using it for years, but not every time. We rotated never letting anyone know for sure where we'd be. It was the way of the world, keeping everyone under radar. Being on radar was never a good thing.

We loaded and hauled ass out of there starting the trek to get this shit done with and get paid.

The ride wasn't too long, and we had no difficulties with the trip.

Pulling up to the warehouse, two cars were in the parking lot along with a large mini-van. Other than that, it was empty, not a single person in sight. Only sporadic trees and shrubbery. Veering off to the side with a roll-up door, Wrong Way parked the truck in a position that all he'd have to do was back up to unload.

Parking, we killed our engines and my mind went through all the different scenarios that could happen. The contingency plans that I had rolling through my head just in case.

If they started shooting when we entered, how we'd fan out to stop it.

If they waited until we got into the building then attacked, how I'd protect my brothers.

Looking at the different escape routes.

Looking for windows, camera, and paths.

Calculating the time it took from point A to point B.

Going over the alternate routes in and out of this warehouse.

Remembering the aerial that Lemon pulled up giving a view of the lay of the land.

All of this filtered through my head as we walked up to the building, Phoenix at the lead, gun at the ready as he opened the door. We followed him, and I was ready for anything. One bullet was all it took, and today wasn't any of my brothers day to bite it.

The building was made of tin, had crates and boxes off to the side walls, and in the center was a large box truck that had some random logo on the side of it. Two men in suits came around the corner. One was light with dark hair, wearing navy blue. The other was tall, olive-toned, and wearing black.

Behind them was another tall man with broad shoulders, tattoos lining his arms. He was obviously the muscle.

I knew two of the names, but not the third. That shit I didn't like either, but we knew there had to be others to get the product switched from one truck to the other. It was a given.

"Crow," the guy with the black suit called out, taking several steps toward us but stopping about ten feet away.

"You are?" I clenched my gun in my hand ready to fire as I watched every single movement the three men made.

"Marcus. Thank you for your help today." He snapped his fingers, and the guy in the navy suit reached into his pocket. All of Ravage raised our guns aiming at the man.

He held his hands up in surrender. "I'm Xavier. I'm reaching in to get your money." I nodded as he slowly did so. There was no bulge of a gun or any weapon. It didn't mean our eyes were lax. He pulled out a large, very well padded envelope and held it out in his hand.

Nodding, Phoenix went and grabbed it coming to stand next to me. Slipping my gun in the back of my jeans, Phoenix standing in front of me as a shield, I opened it and filtered through the bills quickly but efficiently noting the amount was correct.

Handing it off to Wrong Way, he tucked it in the

back of his jeans and slipped his shirt over it along with his cut as Phoenix moved to the side.

"Get this shit off my truck," I ordered.

Wrong Way moved out of the door as we all took steps back. These guys weren't holding guns on us therefore we lowered ours, but kept them in our hands. We weren't taking chances. Trust was built and earned. These two didn't have that yet.

"Calm down. We're not here for trouble," Marcus said calm as could be. "Just want our shit and we're out."

"So, get it," I responded as the large door went up at the side of the building and our truck backed up, stopping just inside the door. The crates were heavy as hell, but we put them in and it was their job to get them out.

Marcus whistled, and two more guys came out and started to empty the truck. We all kept watchful eyes.

A phone sounded, and Xavier pulled it out. "Yeah."

"Fuck." His eyes came to me and whatever it was, it wasn't good. "Yeah, whatever you can," he said, disconnecting.

"We have company. Got guys in a ten-mile radius with eyes. Two white unmarked vans just crossed the ten-mile marker. My guy ran the plates and they're stolen."

Fuck.

Xavier turned to his guys. "Double time. We need out of here in five."

"You get that shit off my truck now or we leave with it," I growled, turning to my brothers. "All of us on our bikes ready." My focus went to Wrong Way quickly going up to him. "Soon as that shit is gone, you pull out and we'll be on ya. If it comes to it, we're out; don't give a fuck if their shit's still on it."

"Right."

I had no fucking clue who these people were, and we didn't know a hundred percent that they were coming for us. A setup could always happen. But fuck if I was taking any chances with my brothers or myself. "What way are they coming? And who are they?" I asked Xavier, looking to my watch and noting the time.

"North and fuck if I know. Once I do, I'll let you know."

I nodded, heading out of the building with my brothers on my heels. "We go south until we know it's clear then head west." The order came out quickly as everyone got on their bikes and waited.

As the seconds ticked by, unease crept up my skin. I hated when that shit happened; it always meant bad things were coming. I needed more bad shit like I needed a hole in my head. Keeping my eyes on Wrong Way, he was watching what was going on in the back of the truck with the camera we had installed and out of the mirrors.

Fuck. We needed to go. Whatever was going on with Xavier and Marcus wasn't our gig, and fuck if I wanted any part of that shit. I had enough on my plate as it was.

Checking my watch, three minutes had passed. Those were some long fucking minutes. Strange how most of the time, life went so fucking fast you couldn't keep up. While other times, like these, it went at a snail's pace.

Firing up my bike and listening to the others revved up beside me, we continued waiting.

That bad feeling was trying to wrap around me like a snake. Looking over to Wrong Way, he caught my eyes as and held up an index finger while I shook my head in the negative. We were done waiting, fuck that and fuck them.

Using my hand to motion, Wrong Way nodded, threw the truck in drive, and took off. I heard the clatter of crates hitting the concrete but didn't give that first fuck.

Wrong Way peeled out of the spot and we followed, noting off to the left through a clearing the two vans coming our way. Fuck that. This shit was their problem not ours.

Gunning it, we were able to get out without a white van in sight.

16

Rylynn

My fingers flitted over the screen typing in the letters quickly. *Made it. Take care of yourself.* Clicking send, it was done. I tossed the phone to my bed and watched it bounce once then settle. He said to call, but something inside of me couldn't do it.

Maybe it was the fact that I had to let him go now. That our time together was finished when I wanted anything but. His life was in Alabama though, not here.

The comment about being on the back of his bike wrapped around my soul. I'd been stupid to think it meant anything but the actual words. There was no hidden meaning he was trying to convey, and I was twisting it in my head. That splash of hope could be a very dangerous thing.

"Get over yourself, Rylynn." Shaking my head, I

grabbed my laptop and responded immediately so I could get paid. She responded immediately. That was one thing off my list to do.

My cell rang, and my belly instantly had flutters. I grabbed for it seeing *Mom* on the screen. "Hey," I answered, disappointment filling me but not showing it.

"Hey yourself. Come over for dinner tonight."

Looking down at the papers scattered all over my living room floor, I replied, "Can we do it another time? I'm working on some things."

"What kind of things?" She pushed, but I wasn't giving her anything.

"Mom."

"You can talk to your father about it."

That wasn't happening. "Relax, Mom."

She coughed. "I made pot roast." I loved my mother's pot roast, it was the best thing to ever come out of a crock pot. The thought of it had my stomach rumbling. "Please come home, Rylynn." Her tone changed from fierce to a bit sad. Her sadness relayed on me.

She was going through the death of her father, and I knew me coming to dinner was just making a point that we were a tight family and there for each other. That we loved each other and appreciated the time we spent together. I needed to give that to her.

"Alright. But I can't stay too long."

"See you at six." She disconnected without hearing

me say bye. Guess she got what she wanted and was done. So be it.

PULLING UP TO THE HOUSE, the sense of home wrapped around me like a warm glove. It had so many memories considering I'd lived here my entire life. The outside got a pick me up with new green siding that my dad installed, but everything else was the same.

The walk up to the front door curved into an L-shape and all the bushes, although a bit bigger, were the same as well.

The tree though, that was the prize. A huge oak tree stood tall in the front yard, so wide around my arms couldn't fit around it. The branches were large and sturdy. Hanging from one of them was a huge tire that my dad said came off an old tractor.

It was my favorite place to be in the world. I'd spun and swung for hours when I lived here, contemplating life and what I wanted to do with it. In that swing was when I decided it was in my blood to help people.

Even with little problems. Since I loved puzzles and solving them, it felt like the right path for me. It ended up being exactly that. I loved what I did, and it all started in that swing.

Jumping down from my Jeep, the front door opened and Mazie darted out of it, running so hard her hair had a hard time catching up with her. "Ry!" she yelled, opening her arms and running right into my stomach. Luckily, I braced or she would've tossed me back with her momentum.

Wrapping my arms around her, she reached my chest already and she was only ten. She was going to pass me up and end up giving me shit about it later in life. A smile came over my lips at the thought.

Loved my baby sister. There was a nine almost ten year gap between us, but to me it didn't matter one bit. Age was just a number. Thoughts of Crow came to me. It was true I had no qualms about age. My father was older than my mother, and they were great together. If you fit, you fit.

She squeezed me hard, and I let the thoughts go. "You've grown like a foot since I last saw you."

She pulled away looking up at me. "You saw me a few days ago."

"When you reach the beanstalk, will you tell me what's up there?"

Mazie smiled. "You know that's not true. Mom said it was a fairy-tale, and we learned in school that fairy-tales aren't real."

What? What kind of teacher would tell a child that shit? They had to believe in something, and it was better that it was good than all the horrible stuff they'd find once they got out into the world. Santa, the tooth fairy—all that shit. It wasn't them per se, it was more of just believing and having that hope of something else out there.

"Who's your teacher so I can put Ex-lax in her coffee?"

Mazie's face scrunched up. "Ex-lax?"

I chuckled. "You know that stuff that makes people poop."

"Ew. You can't give that to Mrs. Crator. She's already mean."

Mazie pulled away taking my hand and leading me up to the house. "Maybe she needs it so she becomes nicer."

She stopped and turned around. "I gave her a Snickers bar. You know like the commercials. One minute people are mad then after they take a bite happy."

The laughter bubbled out. "How'd that go for ya?"

Her little nose scrunched up again. "She ate it, but it didn't help."

She pulled me through the door, and the smell of pot roast filled the air and I sucked it in greedily. I remembered the hundreds of times coming through that exact door after school and smelling it. Then, it made my stomach growl, now, it made it roar.

I cooked, but not a lot. It wasn't that I didn't like to. It was more of a *why when I'm the only one eating* kind of thing. This right here was a treat.

"Baby girl," my dad said, walking into the living

room from the hallway. The floor plan was very simple. When you walked in, you were immediately in the living room, then through a door opening was the kitchen and dining table. Off the kitchen was a hallway that had one bathroom and three bedrooms.

It was small and that's what my mom wanted; therefore, my father loving her more than anything on this planet, gave it to her. She said she wanted all of us close together, but sharing one bathroom sucked at times.

My dad wrapped his beefy arms around me squeezing me tight to him. He smelled of leather and the outdoors. It was unbelievably comforting. Always in his arms I felt safe and protected. It was strange because that same feeling came over me when Crow held me.

He pulled back, but kept ahold of my shoulders. "How are you?" Scary Rhys to everyone else was teddy bear dad to me. Sure he got pissed, but never, not once was I ever afraid of him. Scared he'd take away my phone or Internet access, but never physically.

"Good. Life is good."

His eyes studied me. That was the negative of my father. His gaze was piercing like he could reach inside my brain and pull out all the information that I didn't need him to know. Like he had this superpower, and that I didn't like so much. For me it was the path of least resistance. Not telling him made him not lose his shit over my job because he would. Crow was right about that.

If my father knew exactly what I was doing, he'd get on his Harley and follow me around everywhere. That wouldn't be good.

"Where were you the last couple of days?" His hands fell as he took a step back, crossing his arms over his chest in that dad-way.

"Had to go out of town for a few days. Came back today."

"You didn't think to let your mom and dad know this fact?" he growled, and I knew he was pissed. Here I was almost twenty-years-old and getting lectured by my father. I wasn't going to kid myself and think this part of our relationship was ever going to change. I could be forty, with two kids, husband and dog and he'd still be this way. There was no doubt in my mind about it.

"The Keebler elves called me over to dinner." Holding my father's gaze was hard as hell, but I managed and saw his lip tip.

"You bring me cookies?"

I held out my arms. "Sorry, they only gave me a few and I was hungry. Speaking of hunger." I walked past my father into the kitchen where my mother was stirring what I believed to be gravy on the stove. "Hey, Mom."

A smile was already playing on her lips as she

turned them to me. "No cookies? You know better than that."

I walked up to her back and wrapped my arms around her, her hand coming up to pat my arm. "You'd be surprised how small those cookies actually are. Totally different than what you see in the store."

"I wanna help!" Mazie cried out as my mom looked down to her.

"You can't help with the gravy, it's bubbling and I don't want you burned."

Her arms crossed over her chest and as I looked up, my father had the same pose. "Awe, look it's Dr. Evil and Mini Me."

Mazie turned around to look at our dad, uncrossed her arms and stomped away like she always did when she didn't get her way. I was surprised though, when my father didn't holler at her and tell her she could help. Looked like things were changing and this was good.

Mazie was going to need a heavy hand if she was going to snap out of her being the princess of everything. Time to buck up or the rest of her life wouldn't go well.

"Sit," my dad ordered, pointing to my chair at the table. It was a six seater. My father and mother sat on the ends while Mazie took the spot by Mom and I took the one by Dad.

Not wanting to 'talk,' I said, "I'm gonna help Mom ..."

My father cut me off, hard. "Now, Rylynn."

Looking to my mother, she nodded telling me she had a handle on everything, and I sat in the chair, his gaze intense on me. I knew it was coming, and it was better to get it over with now than let it fester all during the meal.

"Talk to me. Want to know what you're working on."

On a sigh, I rested my elbows on the table, my hands coming up to my mouth. "This isn't a good idea. I know your views on it. You've made them clear as day."

"Want you safe."

Letting my arms fall to the table, I grabbed his hand. It was seriously strong, rough, and calloused. "I am."

"Put it this way. Either tell me or I have a prospect on your ass twenty-four hours a day."

"Is he hot?" I joked, but my father wasn't amused and I knew he wouldn't budge. That was my father, steady as a rock. Always. Huffing out a breath, I answered, "Just two guys whose wives think they're cheating and..." I caught myself, but it was too late because he looked at me expectantly. "A missing girl case. Seventeen. Was at a party and no one has been able to find her."

"Want a man on you."

Leaning back in my chair it was my turn to cross my arms over my chest. "I'm fine. It's mostly research."

"Ry..."

"Dad," I interrupted, "we keep having this same conversation over and over again. I love what I do and with this mystery case, it's a huge puzzle that I'm trying to crack. It's actually fun."

His head shook as he looked up to the ceiling. I was trying his patience, but backing down wasn't an option. This was too important to me to just let it go. This was my passion. No one ever wanted their passion taken away.

Leaning in I lowered my voice. "I'm good at this, and I want you to be happy for me."

His head righted as he leaned into me. "I am happy for you. Just don't want anything to happen to my girl."

Pain crossed his eyes before he wiped it clean. He missed my grandpa, and he didn't want to lose me as well. My grandpa was here with us, I could feel it. I knew he'd be our guardian angel for the rest of our lives, and that made me feel good. To have just a part of him that I carried around with me every single day.

"I am. Promise if it's ever too much that I can't handle, I'll come to you. But right now isn't that time." Hope filled me that he would let this go and we could move on to the eating portion of this interrogation. Loved him, but I wanted this done.

"I'm holding you to that." He leaned back once again and grabbed a bottle of beer from the table taking a swallow. That was when I knew everything was back in the green zone and we could enjoy our meal.

I had this then I needed to check in with Naddy.

A sense of sadness washed over me because Crow entered my mind. It was strange and stupid, but I wanted him here with us, sitting around the table and eating.

It was a thought that would never come true and I squashed it, enjoying a meal with my family.

One thing life had taught me the hard way was to treasure every moment, even the small ones.

17

Crow

"WHO?" I ANSWERED THE PHONE CALL FROM XAVIER instead of a greeting. We'd made it back to Rebellion with no one on our tails or in our business. It didn't mean I let what happened go. We needed to know who the fuck tried to clap in on the shipment. It could be the motherfucker who had eyes on us. Swear to Christ if Tommy fucked us, he was dead.

It was their shipment, but our asses were there too. We needed to cover all of our bases.

"They're dead," he said matter-of-factly.

That was nice, but not what I asked. "Who was it?"

"You don't need to worry. You or your club weren't mentioned in anything."

Anger flooded me as I sat in my office chair stiff. "You're not hearing me. You either tell me who those fuckers were or I come find you." The threat was hard and one I'd follow through on in a heartbeat. All bases would be covered. Always.

He sighed deep on the other end. "We have some issues with one of our runners. He's trying to take over part of our area, and that isn't going to happen."

While he did give me some information, it wasn't enough. "If I have to ask again, Xavier, you'll be having a meeting with my gun."

"I don't appreciate being threatened," he retorted, and I heard my phone give a slight crack as I loosened up my grasp.

"Alright. You wanted it," I challenged, moving to disconnect the phone. Ravage didn't eat shit, and that was what Xavier was trying to shovel our way.

"It was Damien Curtis. He wasn't with them, but we took out seven of his crew who were sent here to take our shipment. How the fuck they knew is something we are working on."

"Yeah, you fucking do that, and I want updates that he's neutralized."

"So this is what I have to look forward to doing business with you?" It was his turn to challenge me, and I didn't give that first flying fuck.

"*If* we decide to do this again. Right now, you'll be lucky to get anything through the Chattanooga."

He sighed again. Xavier had a small business. Growing, but still small for the most part. He needed us more than we needed him. That was always how it was supposed to be. Never count on others, only rely on your brothers.

"Right. I'll get back to you."

"Good." Without another word, I disconnected the phone.

My thumb moved over the screen pulling up my texts. *Made it. Take care of yourself.*

It pissed me off. One, because I wanted to hear her voice over the phone and two, she was saying goodbye, again. I was coming to fucking hate good-byes.

Tossing the phone to the desk, Rylynn was all I could see. Her smartass mouth. Her hair, eyes, and body. How she loved her family and knew about the Ravage history. All of it wrapped into a tall, sexy body.

Closing my eyes, I could smell and taste her. With everything going on, I couldn't go to Sumner right now, but fuck if my hand wasn't itching to spank her ass.

Grabbing my phone, I dialed. She answered on the second ring.

"Hello?"

"Pixie. You didn't call me."

She sighed, and I could picture her face set in a stubborn line. Sexy.

"I texted. That was good enough."

This pissed me off. "No, it wasn't. Needed to make sure you were good. Needed to make sure nothing happened to you. You were on the road for over three hours by yourself. Don't like that shit."

One could hear the laughter in her voice. "Don't worry. I blew two truckers so they would change my tire. It was all good."

Fuck, I loved that smartass mouth. "Guess I'm comin' to Sumner."

She laughed full out. "Oh calm down, Grizzly. I'm good and safe. No worries."

"Good."

I paused on the phone, something on the tip of my tongue to spit out, but it wouldn't come. There was no point in it. And damn if that didn't piss me off too.

"Crow?"

"Yeah, Pixie."

"Thanks for callin'. I appreciate it."

Damn, her voice over the phone was sexy. The way she accentuated different sounds in her words and the fluctuation stood out more over the telephone.

"Yeah, Pixie. I'll call you later."

"Uh... what?"

"I'll call you later."

A heavy knock came to the door just as I heard her starting to make some stupid excuse on why we shouldn't talk on the phone. "Bye," I called out right before I hung up. The next time I talked to her, she'd have a lot to say about that and the anticipation felt like a rush.

"Yeah." The door swung open and Wrong Way stepped through holding a laptop. This wasn't a good sign. Normally, Wrong Way didn't bring his computer to me. This could only mean one thing. "You found something."

"Yep." He brought the computer to the side of my desk, set it down, grabbed a chair, and pulled it over next to me. On the screen was a large detailed spreadsheet.

Wrong Way started punching some keys. "Carlo is taking money off the top before he puts it in the safe. I went through every roll of receipts to find out how he was doing it, and it started to add up. The differences." He turned it to me, and my stomach clenched.

In bold red numbers, it said one hundred thousand, seven hundred fifty-six dollars and some change. "You're fuckin' shittin' me. Please tell me you're shittin' me."

"Sorry, boss. But nope. Going through the receipts and the bank statements with a fine-toothed comb—with taking our other *stuff* out, that's what it comes up to being lost. He's a smart motherfucker. Not taking too much at one time. A little here. A little there. Enough that it wouldn't send us on alert, but also enough for him to make it worth his while."

"You know for sure it was him?" While I knew Wrong Way wouldn't bring me this shit unless it was true, I had to ask since I intended on putting a bullet between his eyes. Knowing he was really the fucker who did was necessary.

Without hesitation, he pulled up the feed from the store on the computer. Blackness covered the screen for a moment. "He covered up the camera in the office." Sure enough, it shows exactly when Carlo pulled the covering down, even smiling into it with a shit-eating grin. Fucking prick. "Now this." He pulled up footage outside the office door.

It showed Carlo going in. Wrong Way paused it. "See right there." He pointed to the screen that had a side view of Carlo, one hand in his right pocket.

"Yeah."

"Watch this."

On the screen was Carlo coming out of the office. Wrong Way paused it then pointed to the same pocket. It currently had no hand in it and it was bulging.

"Fucker. Any idea how long it's been goin' on?"

"About five months, but the first two of those, it wasn't much. He was watching to see if I'd catch it, but it was so small and since I don't do the checks from the receipts only the books, I missed it. Also, pulled his bank information." The screen turned to a bank statement. "We paid him on Fridays with direct deposit. Here it shows that the money went through. Those are the only deposits he's made."

"Therefore, he has our money somewhere liquid."

"Yep. That'd be my guess."

"Now on, you're on the books at the store watching the receipts and cash in. Every month, after we find

Carlo's replacement, you go there and make sure all the numbers add up with the receipts. We do not need the feds or the state after us for something this stupid, when we can get it handled right now."

"Got it, boss."

"Wait. Did you find anything out at the Purple Pride?"

"Been swamped in this. That'll be my next go."

"Good. Round up the guys. We're goin' fishin'."

Wrong Way chuckled as I grabbed my phone, seeing I hadn't closed the text from Rylynn. This time it made me smile. She thought she could run, but she couldn't. Only time would tell.

I checked my guns, added a few more, and met my brothers outside the club. Giving them a brief low down, needless to say everyone was pissed as we took off down the road, only a few minutes later pulling up to Carlo's home.

His car wasn't in the drive giving us the perfect opportunity to check out his house. We ended up parking around the side of the house, took off our cuts, and walked up to the door like we were supposed to be there. That was a very important thing that people always forgot. If your head was held high and you looked like you belonged somewhere, no one would question you.

They'd go on their way not giving you a second thought.

If you're timid and shaky, that puts a fucking bull's-eye on your back. No one needed that shit.

Instead of busting down the door, Brewer pulled out his tools and had the lock popped in seconds as we noted the people on their porches. Since we looked like we belonged there and Phoenix did his crazy-ass welcome like last time, no one said a word as we entered.

"This doesn't have to be pretty," I told them with only one thing on my mind—wanting our fucking money back. Hell, we all did.

"Now that's what I'm talkin' about." Phoenix pulled out his knife and began slitting through the cushions of the couch. The guys spread out through the house. Dishes could be heard breaking on the floor in the kitchen and different crashes throughout the house. I tossed a few pictures off the walls seeing nothing behind them.

"Crow!" Rooster called out, stepping into the hallway and waving me once in his direction. Entering the room, the floor boards were popped up under the bed. It was good too because it only showed about a fourth of an inch above the rest of the floor. Rooster had great eyes.

Rooster pulled the board back and pulled out its confines. "Fuck. He's that stupid to put the cash in a Ziploc bag?"

He nodded, opened the bag, and started counting. It would take him a while.

"What the…" I heard in the distance, then a scuffle, then a solid punch being thrown and connecting on someone's body. Darting out of the room, Phoenix's knee was in the small of Carlo's back on the floor with Brewer aiming his gun at the man's head. Bags of food were scattered all over the floor, apples rolling this way and that, cracked eggs leaking all over the floor.

"Seems we have a problem." My boot pressed down on the side of his face as he began yelling and trying to get loose from Phoenix with absolutely no luck at all. "You see. We pay you to do a job. Very well I might add." I pressed down harder feeling the push back from his jawbone. "And you stole from us. That was a stupid mistake, Carlo."

Picking up my boot, I used every bit of strength and slammed it down on the asshole's face hitting directly on his jaw. He cried out in pain, but my boot was far from the worst of his problems. "Get him up." Phoenix did as asked and Carlo had a difficult time keeping to his feet.

"I didn't…" the asshole started with a mumble unable to move his jaw right, but I didn't want to hear a fucking thing. My fist connected with his jaw on the opposite side, his head flying to the side. My leather gloves protected me from his blood now oozing out of his mouth on both sides.

"Rooster!" I yelled, and the man came through the hallway into the living room. "All there?"

"Lookin' like it. Don't know how but he's got bigger bills in it making it easier to count." That I didn't give one shit about. If it was our money, didn't matter what bills they were.

"Now... what do we do with a thief?"

My brothers all looked at each other, a smile on their faces. This wasn't my favorite part of the job, but it was necessary. Brewer, Lemon, and Hornet dragged Carlo to the kitchen and laid his hands on the counter top. Tex stuffed a rag in Carlo's mouth to shut him up. No need to alert the neighbors.

This was Phoenix's gig. He got off on it.

"You have sticky fingers, taking what's not yours." I nodded to Phoenix who held his knife his focus now on Carlo.

Phoenix pressed the blade down on his pinky finger. Blood spattered the counter tops and floor.

Carlo's screams were muffled as he tried to get away, but it didn't work. There was no running from Ravage. He knew what he was getting himself into when he started this. Now he suffered the conse-quences of his actions.

One by one each of Carlo's fingers were removed. On the seventh one, he passed out. We tried waking him up, but it didn't work. Phoenix shrugged. "Bullet and get him buried."

"I hate the diggin' part," Lemon groaned, and Rooster slapped him upside the head.

"Then call a prospect and have them do it, dumbass."

"You fuckin' hit me again we got problems," Lemon challenged, and we didn't need this shit right now. We needed to get our business done and get out.

"Knock that shit off. Wrong Way, get the van and pull it into the garage. Get the body in the back and get him underground." Wrong Way took off. "We secure it. Brewer, you're here tonight and light it up."

It was Brewer's turn to smile. He was a pyro fanatic. Knew everything there was to know about explosives. Shit that no one should have in their arsenal, yet he did. Growing up together, he hadn't changed one bit.

"Just another day in paradise," Rooster said, clapping his hand on my shoulder.

"Right."

"WHY IN THE hell is something as fine as her with a dick like him?" Brewer asked from the passenger seat of my Tahoe as we sat in front of Sophia's house. He was snapping pictures. I was watching how the asshole acted with Sophia.

That snake slithered up my skin once again telling me something was wrong. Maybe it was her having a man, but it had been too long for the jealousy card to be played. No. It was the guy.

"According to what Lemon pulled up, he works at the lumber yard and has a place in the town over. He's been seein' Sophia for about three weeks." Which made me wonder why in the fuck this guy was taking in boxes.

Sophia wouldn't let the asshole move in... at least that was what I thought. When a large suitcase came out of the back of the dick's truck, it stuck the nail in the coffin. That asshole was going to be in a house with my kid. It was time to dig down deep with this guy.

"People make decent money at the yard, but that truck is brand new, Crow. Costs over forty-five K. That's a lot on his salary."

"Alright. Call Ethan and have him tail this fuckwad. I want to know everything from the time he wakes up until he goes to bed and while he's sleepin'."

Brewer pulled out his phone and made the call.

Oh Sophia, what have you gotten yourself into?

MUSIC BOOMED through the clubhouse so loud it could be heard outside where I sat by the pool. It was the prime spot to see the women leaving nothing to the imagination. Brewer sat next to me taking slow pulls off his beer.

Looking out among the people the sense of family overtook me. I was an only child, and all of these people filled in that gap for me. Family wasn't blood. It was those who had your back through the thick and thin of life. These men around me were my family, down to my soul.

I'd do anything to protect them, and they would do the same.

While there were lots of people who didn't understand the MC lifestyle, I didn't really get not being in it. Loyalty among people these days was a lost cause. Everyone trying to one up the next and spent their lives doing that shit.

There were no rules out there when it came to people, but in here there was and we followed them to the letter. Loyalty, trust, and commitment to the club and brothers were the top priority. We stood by that and would stand by that for as long as this club was around.

"You find anything about Damien yet?" I asked Brewer.

He shook his head. "I'm thinkin' it's an alias, but I've got Lemon on it."

Before I could respond Ethan came up. "Got a minute?"

Waving my hand out, I invited him to sit. "Been on that guy for two days now. He doesn't work in the lumber yard. He drove right past it both days heading south into Stagnant. Crow, he went into the Purple Pride." This place had to be something. How could this place show up with a man we were trying to find, Barry, and my ex's man?

"Wrong Way find anything out there?" Brewer asked.

I shook my head. "He was too caught up in the books and Carlo. It was his next project."

"Looks like you might want to move that along," Brewer added.

"Ya think. Find him, tell him what's going on. He needs to get his ass over to Stagnant and find out what the fuck is going on there. Make sure someone has his back."

Brewer nodded just as my cell rang, and he halted. I pulled it out of the pocket inside my cut. The call said, *Cruz calling.* I sat up straight, Brewer catching my movement his eye acute.

"What?" he asked.

"Cruz's callin' me." I took the call. "Crow."

"Need you in Sumner by tomorrow night," Cruz said, abrupt and strange. He was a hard man, but he always at least said hi or this is Cruz.

"Why?" Rising from the chair, I moved off into the distance where the music was muffled so I could hear clearer. This was obviously important. Leaning against the fence, my leg bent at the knee, foot landing on the wood.

"Tomorrow. Need you here."

"You're not gonna tell me why?"

The other end of the phone was silent for a few beats. "Just get here by tomorrow night."

"Are you okay?"

"Yeah. Club's good, just need to talk to you. Comin'?"

I flipped my watch checking out the time, for what reason I didn't know. It wasn't like I'd leave tonight to make the trip there. And there... Rylynn was there.

"Yep."

"Good." He hung up the phone, and I walked back over to Brewer.

"What was that about?" he asked with curious eyes.

"Cruz wants me in Sumner by tomorrow night. Wouldn't tell me why."

Brewer sat up straight, then moved to get up and stand next to me. "That's strange. You want me to get the guys together?"

"Just you and Wrong Way. Pull Wrong Way off the Purple Pride and get Phoenix and Tex to go. Explain why we need this intel. Everyone else needs to stay here, get shit done, and keep their eyes open. Also, get Phoenix to make a visit to Tommy as soon as possible. We need the guys to rotate at the store and have Hornet find a replacement for Carlo on the double."

"Right."

"Get your shit together, we're headin' to Sumner in the morning."

That slithery snake crawled up my back, warning me. This meeting felt off, and I hoped I was fucking wrong about that and it didn't change my world forever.

18

Rylynn

ELIZABETH. ELIZABETH. ELIZABETH. WHERE ARE YOU?
Reading through the files, I thought for sure they'd be
seared in my brain soon enough.

Since the party was still going on when the police
arrived, they cited several of the attendees with
underage drinking while questioning them about Elizabeth's whereabouts. Normally cops would wait forty-
eight hours for a missing person, but an underage
party trumped that.

After I called Naddy upon leaving my parents'
house, she express mailed to me a flash drive that she
said I needed to see.

Placing it in my laptop it loaded. I clicked on the
little boxes and then the stupid ones that ask you if this
shit is safe or not. Could never be too careful these
days I guessed.

My breathing stopped for a moment. It was video surveillance from inside the Walps' home where the party was held.

It took hours to get through the entire thing. I watched Elizabeth go into the bathroom and then she never came out. There was a window in there, which had to mean she snuck out through there. *Did the cops print the window?* She couldn't have just vanished. The window was her only way out.

I searched through the police reports coming up short. That was strange. One would think that would be a top priority considering it was the only way she could've gotten out. Then I pulled out the large list of evidence and went through every line item to see if the prints were on there. It wasn't. That piece of the puzzle didn't fit.

Rewatching the clips where Elizabeth was shown, I ignored her and watched the people around her, matching pictures in the file to those on the screen. Three boys showed on the screen during different times at the party, but I didn't have an interview sheet from the police on them. Those were the three I needed to talk to. I still hadn't been able to catch Penny at her house and my searches were coming up blank, but I kept trying.

My heart bled for these parents, not knowing where their daughter was. The feeling was new to me because before Grandpa there wasn't a loved one who had left us. They'd been living this nightmare for months; it was worse in a way.

At least with Grandpa, we knew what happened to him. We knew when he left us. These parents had nothing but a pile of papers that led nowhere near their daughter. The pain they must have felt, I understood.

The alarm on my phone went off. Shit. I left everything scattered on my floor since this wouldn't take long. It was time to take some more pictures of pony play husband and get this one off my list. Depending on if a new case came in or not, the missing girl would be my top priority.

Grabbing my camera and bag, I set off to watch a horse get him some.

19

Crow

THE RIDE WAS GREAT INTO SUMNER WITH THE SUN SHINE following us there. There were no hiccups along the way, and I had all my guys doing what needed to be done back home, but I still had no idea why I was being summoned here.

The sense of unease rode on my shoulders the entire way there though, and grew stronger when we hit the *Welcome to Sumner* sign and entered the town.

Ideas of why I was there went rampant through my brain, but nothing stood out more than anything else. Considering I saw Cruz at Dagger's funeral and he said nothing at that time, whatever this was happened recently. Since the only thing I did while in Sumner was fuck Rylynn, it might be about that. But if that were true, wouldn't it be Rhys calling me instead? Way too many questions with no answers.

I was here now so I imagined I would soon find out what this was about.

Pulling up to the clubhouse, the gate opened immediately and we glided into a parking spot, killing the bikes and getting off.

Buzz, Breaker, Cooper, Deke and Rhys were all there to greet me and ushered me inside to Cruz's office. Rhys didn't punch me so it being about Rylynn was a no. With a chin lift to my guys, I entered the room where Cruz stood up from the desk, shook my hand, and gave me a one armed man back-slap in greeting. This was the same as any other time I'd caught up with him.

"What's goin' on?"

He sat in his seat. "Have a seat," he said and I did, crossing my ankles. We were alone in the room with the door shut. Therefore, it for sure had nothing to do with the club as a whole.

His face was a mask not giving anything away. Wouldn't lie and say it put me at ease. Cruz was a stand up man. That I knew for fact. When his eyes connected with mine, something swirled in my gut. No, this wasn't going to be pretty.

"Recently I came into possession of some information. Since I didn't know one hundred percent if it was true, I had it looked into. Deeply."

"Okay..." The word was drawn out. It looked as though he was trying to steady his breath, which was strange because Cruz did what he wanted, said what he wanted, and didn't give a fuck what anyone thought. That slither got faster at his change in demeanor.

"It has to do with you." My knees cocked as my back straightened while Cruz ran his hand through his hair. "There's no easy way to say this shit, and it fuckin' kills me to tell you it."

My heart rate escalated as I waited for the bomb of whatever had him looking and acting like that dropped. Shit, was it about my dad or a member of my club?

He held out a folder which I took, but still kept my focus on him, the folder feeling like a lead weight drawing my hand to lay on my lap. Whatever was in this was big. Trying to run the different scenarios in my head didn't work since I knew nothing.

Cruz nodded to the folder. Pain struck across his features surprising the shit out of me. But nothing. Nothing could've prepared me for what he said next. "In there, you will find a DNA test ran that states—I'm your biological father."

I rose swift to my feet clenching the information in my hand, anger, confusion, and fear all colliding. "That's not fuckin' possible. You know my dad. He's buddies with yours. There's no fuckin' way this is possible."

Cruz took in a deep breath standing from his chair as well. "Believe me. I'm as shocked as you are with this. Know you and your dad are tight. No way do I want to fuck that up, but I needed you to know. This isn't the kind of shit that I push aside. Your mother is Alma Moore, correct." I nodded, trying not to come out of my skin, which was barely holding on by a thread. "She was around our club before going to Rebellion. This was about four years before Cooper was born. We had a fling, and she disappeared. Never thought anything of it. Women came and went all the time through those clubhouse doors. Except come to find out, she had my baby inside of her when she took off. There are pictures in there of your mom and I together. It wasn't a relationship, but we fucked a few times."

"This isn't right." My head shook, all the possibilities floating through my mind, my world turning upside down. Confusion was winning out over everything else.

"Open the papers," he ordered. It was my turn to suck in a breath. My body was strung tight, but I got it under control. I sat and opened the folder not wanting to, but needed to in the same breath. "Your DNA was in the system from when you were young and got arrested. Don't think your dad knew the cops took it, but they did and classified it. What I'm thinking is the cops knew you were a son of a Ravage member and took it while they could. Had to do some troubleshooting, but we got it open. Had it run with mine and it was a match."

Christ. This could not be possible. It just couldn't.

As I looked at the papers one said Caleb Moore-Blaine while the other side said Donovan Cruz. It showed it was a positive match at ninety-nine-point-nine percent. Fuck, didn't think one could get much closer than that.

Fuck. Everything in my life had been one big fucking lie after the other. The man who raised me really had no claim to me. Did he know this or did my mother dupe him in to taking me on all my life?

There were so many questions I had for my dad, but obviously, that had to wait. Fuck. When I said my dad, I'd meant the one in Rebellion. As of right now, Cruz was just my brother. I couldn't wrap my head around being his kid just yet.

It was like a bomb ready to explode busting me to shit.

I was thrown off. The world was spinning out of control. I was out of control. I moved around the chair, hand to my chin as I walked around needing to do something besides just stand there like an oaf. "Well, my mother was a piece of shit, so it wouldn't surprise me if she did this." My anger grumbled out through my words reaching new heights. It was as if a switch flipped inside of me cranking my anger up higher than it had ever been before. It was so much my hand started shaking.

I hated my mother.

She was a worthless whore who used me to play my dad... who wasn't even my dad. The betrayal cut me to the core. How would he take this? What did he know?

My entire life was playing on a reel in my mind.

I had to get out of here and have time to process what was going on. I had to feel the air on my face and sun on my body.

I blew out a deep breath trying to contain my emotions. Closing my eyes, a vision of an angel came clearly to my head. Everything settled seeing her smirk, her body, her face.

Rylynn.

Hell, I needed Rylynn, but I hadn't called her wanting to surprise her at her place after this. Now, I needed her. All of this was so far out in left field it would've never been on any contingency plan I thought up. There was no preparing for this kind of news. I came here thinking it was another day and another club situation.

This shit was personal.

As personal as it could get.

The ground underneath me was shaking so profusely, threatening to sink me further into the pain swirling around me. Anger and pain seemed to go hand in hand, but it couldn't happen. There was too much at stake. One, Cruz ran the entire MC and two, he looked about as devastated as I did shocking the shit out of me.

"Know this is hard. It is for me too. It come out of nowhere and I swear if I'd have known about you, you would've been with me."

My steps faltered. "Except the thing is, I was happy right where I landed." The words tumbled out. My instincts screamed to tell him he didn't know how good I had it. My dad was a good father. He was the reason I was the man I was today. He was everything. Instead, I just watched the man in front of me.

"That's good. I don't want to come into your life and barge all over it. It'll be hard not to, but this situation is jacked up and we need time to sort it out."

"Gotta go. Need time to process this." I headed to the door. I had to get out. The walls were closing in.

Cruz nodded. "Are you gonna stay in town?"

"No."

Cruz's head fell, and every feeling inside me was so jumbled I couldn't process it. Clutching the papers, the pain ripped through me tearing me from one end to the other. The pain of having a father I never knew about. The pain of having a father that had been the best one ever. Pain that my anger was so rampant it physically hurt. Pain that everything I'd known my entire life was a lie. Everything. From the moment I was conceived till the day I stood in this very spot in Cruz's office.

Clutching the door handle, I spoke, "Don't know where this goes from here. But what I do know is I have a dad at home. A damn good one. No way in hell I'd ever shit on him. And I don't know how I feel about you and me. Need time." With that, I turned the handle and got out of that office.

The Sumner brothers that were around watched as I walked through the clubhouse. Not a single one stopped me. Judging from their faces, they already knew. Lifting my chin to them, I got outside and started up my bike. Wrong Way and Brewer came fast getting on their rides.

One glance up and I saw a wide-eyed Rylynn. She was here and just by looking at her, my heart squeezed painfully. I needed her now more than ever. I needed her warmth to push away all the darkness that crept up on me.

Our eyes locked.

Connected.

She read me.

I gave her that in a single glance because she was Rylynn and this was us.

She moved quick not looking at anyone but me. Rylynn hopped on the back of my bike and wrapped her arms around me tight.

It was exactly what I needed.

Her.

She came freely. No questions. No judgments. One

look, one connection, one pain, and she gave me everything I needed in this moment.

One last look at the people standing outside, Rhys stood there a mask of fury. Rylynn wasn't fazed. She was with me without hesitation.

Life threw you curveballs. I'd just had mine in Cruz's office.

Rhys obviously just had his. Thinking on the life we led, I was sure he never thought he'd see the day his daughter rode off with the likes of me. That was for another day, though. I couldn't stay here right now.

What I needed was the open road to clear my mind. What I needed was to sink inside Rylynn and forget where I ended and she began. What I needed had her arms wrapped around my waist and the beast of my bike under our bodies.

Everyone else, club and all be damned.

We took off through the gates. With every twist of the throttle, I had one goal in mind—get the hell out of Sumner. Get away from it all.

The only thing keeping me upright on my bike was Rylynn. It was that moment when I knew things had changed.

Welcome to my fucked up life, Rylynn.

Because no matter what was up or down in my world, she was mine, and I wasn't letting go.

THE STORY CONTINUES in Fueled in Fire releasing on November 27th. Preorder TODAY!

Please read below.

HELLO! It's Ryan.

I know. I know. I did it to you. Don't hate me please!

I never set out to leave you with a cliffhanger. Connected in Pain was always going to be one book. Then with the new club, new members, old members, ol' ladies and everything in-between, there was a lot to explore and so many different avenues to go down. Then add in the fact that Rylynn and Crow just wouldn't shut the hell up, the book became its own beast.

No matter what I did or how I changed things, I couldn't condense their story into one book and give it the justice it needed.

The good news is you don't have to wait long for the next book!

It will come out on November 27th. Don't forget to preorder.

Hope you love Rylynn and Crow's story as much as I did writing it!

~Ryan

PREORDER TODAY!

The story continues in Fueled in Fire releasing on November 27th. Preorder TODAY!

ACKNOWLEDGMENTS

To my readers: Thank you so much for reading Connected in Pain. You're the reason I'm able to write these stories and bring them to life. Words will never be enough to show my gratitude to you, just know you're in my heart and appreciate you.

Critique Partner: Chelsea Camaron, thank you for putting up with all my shit. The questions, the bitching, the frustration—you take all of it, and keep me on track. You're the best.

Beta Readers: Kimberly, you're awesome. Bet you never thought our meeting at a signing would lead you into the twisted world of the creative process of my books. Ha!! Thank you for all your help. You kick ass at finding those small details that slip my mind (which let's just say are A LOT). You're the greatest. Thank you.

SM Donaldson, you rock. Even without power and so much going on in your life, you took time out to read CIP for me and give me feedback. I adore you, thank you so much.

Cola, surprise! Met you thought CC and stole you! Just kidding. :) Thank you so much for helping me with this book and for being there at the drop of a hat for me.

HUGE thank you to Silla Webb, my editor. You are always there when I need you. I never have to worry with you and you have my eternal gratitude.

Cassy, my cover designer. Thank you for putting up with my shit load of changes when it comes to the covers. In the end, you design the best ones. You're always there ready to help and I greatly appreciate it.

Wander, my photographer for Connected in Pain. Thank you! The image is amazing and fits the story perfectly you. You and Andrey rock!

Nate, thank you for being the perfect Crow.

OTHER BOOKS WRITTEN BY RYAN MICHELE

www.authorryanmichele.com/books

Ravage MC Series
Ravage Me
Seduce Me
Consume Me
Inflame Me
Captivate Me
Ravage MC Novella Collection
Ravage MC Box Set

Bound by Ravage: A Taste of the Ravage MC

Ravage MC Bound Series
Bound by Family
Bound by Desire

Bound by Vengeance

Bound by Affliction

Bound by Destiny

Bound by Wreckage

Bound by Destruction

Ravage MC Rebellion Series

Connected in Pain

Fueled in Fire

Power Chain: Anti-Hero Game

Power Chain

PowerHouse

Power Player

PowerLess

Overpowered

Vipers Creed MC

Crossover

Challenged

Conquering

Ruthless Rebels MC

Shamed

Scorned

Scarred

Schooled

Ruthless Rebels Box Set

Raber Wolf Pack Series

Raber Wolf Pack Book 1
Raber Wolf Pack Book 2
Raber Wolf Pack Book 3
Raber Wolf Pack Series Box Set

Standalone Romances

Full Length Novels

Needing to Fall
Safe
Wanting You
Blood & Loyalties: A Mafia Romance

Novellas

Stood Up (Billionaire Up Romance)

Short Stories

Hate to Love
Branded
Bangin'

www.authorryanmichele.com/books

ABOUT THE AUTHOR

Ryan Michele found her passion in bringing fictional characters to life. She loves being in an imaginary world where anything is possible, and she has a knack for special twists readers don't see coming.

She writes MC, Contemporary, Erotic, Paranormal, New Adult, Inspirational, and other romance-based genres. Whether it's bikers, wolf-shifters, mafia, etc., Ryan spends her time making sure her heroes are strong and her heroines match them at every turn.

When she isn't writing, Ryan is a mom and wife, living in rural Illinois and reading by her pond in the warm sun.

Join my Reader Group: Ryan's Sultry Sinners

Sign Up for my Newsletter

Come find me:
www.authorryanmichele.com
ryanmicheleauthor@gmail.com

facebook.com/authorryanmichele

twitter.com/Ryan_Michele

instagram.com/author_ryan_michele

bookbub.com/authors/ryan-michele

Thank you for reading!

Ryan
Michele

Made in the USA
Middletown, DE
31 July 2020

14103037R00165